Dear Romance Reader,

Welcome to a world of breathtaking passion and never-ending romance.
Welcome to *Precious Gem Romances*.

It is our pleasure to present *Precious Gem Romances*, a wonderful new line of romance books by some of America's best-loved authors. Let these thrilling historical and contemporary romances sweep you away to far-off times and places in stories that will dazzle your senses and melt your heart.

Sparkling with joy, laughter, and love, each *Precious Gem Romance* glows with all the passion and excitement you expect from the very best in romance. Offered at a great affordable price, these books are an irresistible value—and an essential addition to your romance collection. Tender love stories you will want to read again and again, *Precious Gem Romances* are books you will treasure forever.

Look for fabulous new *Precious Gem Romances* each month—available only at Wal★Mart.

Kate Duffy
Editorial Director

Books by Lisa Plumley

SURRENDER
THE HONEYMOON HOAX
MY BEST FRIEND'S BABY
TIMELESS SPRING
TIMELESS WINTER
OUTLAW
LAWMAN
HER BEST MAN

Published by Kensingon/Zebra Books

MAN OF THE YEAR

Lisa Plumley

Zebra Books
Kensington Publishing Corp.
http://www.zebrabooks.com

ZEBRA BOOKS are published by

Kensington Publishing Corp.
850 Third Avenue
New York, NY 10022

Copyright © 2000 by Lisa Plumley

All rights reserved. No part of this book may be reproduced in any form or by any means without the prior written consent of the Publisher, excepting brief quotes used in reviews.

If you purchased this book without a cover you should be aware that this book is stolen property. It was reported as "unsold and destroyed" to the Publisher and neither the Author nor the Publisher has received any payment for this "stripped book."

Zebra and the Z logo Reg. U.S. Pat. & TM Off.

First Printing: July, 2000
10 9 8 7 6 5 4 3 2 1

Printed in the United States of America

*To my husband, John,
who makes hills and oceans possible,
brings laughs to the hard times,
and is always ready with the champagne.
(Thanks, honey!)*

One

Things had a way of working out for Paige Mulvaney . . . at least in her imagination.

Like this morning's job interview. On the way, she'd survived an unseasonably rainy Arizona summer morning with only minor muddy spots on her navy pumps. She'd arrived at SupraTech, Saguaro Vista's most well-known and—more importantly to Paige—most innovative high-tech company, with almost fifteen minutes to spare before her interview. And she'd managed to slip into the posh ladies' room near the lobby before anyone noticed the enormous, gaping hole in her pantyhose.

Could she be any luckier?

Well, she could if she snagged this engineering job, Paige told herself. It would be the perfect finale to her years of studying, research, and preparation. It would be the cherry atop the sundae of her intellectual career . . . it would be the cream cheese on the bagel of her lifelong academic pursuits, it would be . . . No. This had to stop. She really should have taken time for breakfast this morning. Now, between her rumbling stomach and overeager imagination, food seemed to be all she could think of.

This just wouldn't do. Concentrating her thoughts on the appointment to come, Paige propped her briefcase on the ladies' room sink and bent to survey the damage to her interview outfit.

Raindrops spattered her navy business suit. The collar of her white blouse sagged from a combination of age and humidity. Further down, a good portion of her right knee was exposed by the rip in her pantyhose, caused by an unfortunate encounter with one of the overdue rental videotapes littering her roommate's car—which Paige had been forced to borrow, when hers had failed to start this morning.

Now that she'd arrived, though, things were starting to look up. Or at least they were bound to. Soon. She checked her watch. Only a few minutes to go. With sudden decisiveness, Paige ducked into one of the stalls, peeled off her pantyhose, and stuffed them into her briefcase. That accomplished, she examined her appearance in the mirror with critical eyes.

The same plain face she was used to stared back at her. On the bright side, her suit and briefcase and shoes—even without pantyhose—presented exactly the no-nonsense impression she needed to get a foot in the door at a company like SupraTech. And that was what mattered. Once she was hired, she would be able to prove to her parents once and for all that their efforts on behalf of their only daughter hadn't gone to waste.

Buoyed by the thought, Paige gathered her things and strode toward her future, trying not to wince at the loud clip-clopping of her heels against the tiled lobby floor.

In the SupraTech reception area, the woman behind the elegant curved desk looked up with a smile.

"Good morning," she said. "How may I help you?"

"I'm here for the open interview." Knees knocking, Paige withdrew a copy of her résumé and the classified ad she'd clipped from the Sunday *Arizona Territorial*. She slid both across the desk.

The receptionist read the ad. Absently, she shoved back a lustrous hank of long blond hair, then looked up. Her gaze traveled the length of Paige's suit, then returned to her face.

"You're here for the interview?" She tapped the clipping. *"This* interview?"

"Of course." Paige looked at the classified ad again, just to make sure she hadn't grabbed one of her roommate's beloved yard sale clippings instead. She hadn't. The ad was the same one she remembered from yesterday—the one she'd seized on with the mysterious, unshakable certainty that this was an opportunity tailor-made for her.

Find out what's in store for you at SupraTech, it read. *High-profile positions available now—open interviews to be conducted.*

She skimmed over the remaining details about the dates and times. Yes, this was definitely it. Her chance to put her triple degrees in computer engineering, economics, and industrial engineering to good use. As a private, family owned company, SupraTech didn't open its doors to job applicants very often. This was a great chance. And Paige meant to take advantage of it.

"There must be some mistake." The receptionist frowned in puzzlement. "The interviews are . . ." She trailed off, gesturing vaguely toward a hallway and an adjacent bank of elevators.

Paige frowned toward the elevators, then caught on. "I realize I'm a little early. I hope that's all right."

"Oh, it's . . . fine."

The receptionist eyed Paige's interview suit again, giving it a look that made Paige wish she could tattoo her IQ on her forehead. At least then her best asset would be in plain view.

"Why don't you have a seat?" the woman asked, picking up the phone. "I'll just double-check with Mrs. Richardson."

Nora Richardson. SupraTech's founder and famous CEO. With a twinge of excitement, Paige mumbled her thanks and retreated to the seating area. She was almost in!

In an effort to hide her nervousness, she opened her briefcase and scanned her résumé, then double-checked the technical specifications she'd written for the new projects she hoped to work on if she got hired. She had several presentations all ready to go. She'd rehearsed them with her roommate just last night, between bowls of microwave popcorn and batches of double-cheese nachos with jalapeños.

Mmmm. Nachos. Unwanted visions of junk food rose in her mind, taunting her with images of salty snacks, chocolate chip cookies, and bowls brimful with jelly beans. Shifting in her chair, Paige blinked and focused on her papers. She might be called for her interview at any minute, and she couldn't afford to be caught daydreaming.

Five minutes and one caramel apple fantasy later, the receptionist still hadn't summoned her. Enough was enough, even for the sort of well-mannered person Paige considered herself to be. Summoning her courage, she tucked everything back into her briefcase and snapped it shut, preparing to assert herself.

She hoped she wouldn't have to.

Just as she stood, a tall, dark-haired man breezed through the lobby and past her. Startled, Paige tumbled back onto the sofa, dropping her briefcase on the cushions. She corralled it, slapped it against her lap, and looked up.

The source of her troubles had already arrived at the receptionist's desk. He leaned against it and grinned at the blonde. "Hey, Jennifer. Is she in?" He waved his arm toward the hallway and the elevators. For the first time, Paige noticed the subtle indentation of an office door at the far end of the area.

"Sure, Brodie. She's always in for you," the receptionist told him. She gave him, Paige couldn't help but notice, a look much warmer than she herself had earned.

"Thanks. You're terrific." He leaned closer— Paige did, too—and said something else in a low voice. A giggle burbled up from the blonde. Then the man tweaked one of her long curls, turned, and strode toward the doorway in question.

Halfway there, the receptionist's voice rang out again. "Hang on a sec," Jennifer warned. "I wouldn't go in there if I were you."

"Oh, no." He skidded to a stop, swiveling back toward the reception area desk. "Don't tell me."

The receptionist nodded. "Yup."

"She's at it again?"

"Afraid so."

"Oh, no." The sudden expression that crossed his face was almost enough to make Paige feel guilty for eavesdropping on his conversation with the blonde.

Almost.

After all, nothing this dramatic ever happened to anyone like her. Not in real life.

Looking trapped, the man called Brodie turned in a circle. He wore scuffed athletic sandals and Paige let her gaze travel upward from those sandals, over nicely tanned male legs, and higher. His brightly colored baggy shorts were hardly corporate attire. Neither were the sunglasses in his hand and the wrinkled white T-shirt stretched across his shoulders. But none of that really mattered. Because underneath them all was one of the most gorgeous men she'd ever seen up close.

Not even his unshaven chin could disguise that fact. Nor could his shaggy dark hair, badly in need of a cut but somehow managing to seem stylish, all the same. He looked, Paige decided, like one of those trendily mussed male models—all rugged angles, tight muscles, and world-weary attitude.

She stifled a sigh and made herself quit gawking. Men like this one, like this Brodie person, never noticed her. No point making a spectacle of herself. Especially not when she had more important matters to attend to, such as her overdue interview. Newly determined, Paige tightened her sweaty grasp on her briefcase handle, drew in a deep breath, and rose again from the sofa.

The motion drew the man's attention, and his face turned toward hers. For one startling instant, she felt the force of all his considerable charisma . . . focused on *her*. The impact of it was enough to make an ordinary girl blush.

It made a certified wallflower like Paige freeze in miserable self-consciousness. Awkwardly, she stopped halfway up, willing herself to look calm. Cool. Collected. She gave him her best attempt at a carefree smile, and straightened all the way. And then the unthinkable happened . . . he walked toward her.

He hoped she hadn't recognized him. Brodie strode toward the mousy brunette beside the sofa. As soon as most women figured out who he was, they lost their cool, one way or the other. Then came the seductive whispers and the notes with lipstick prints and phone numbers. Embarrassing invitations. Hotel room keys had been slipped into his pockets. And—when he had turned down other, more tempting offers—the requests for autographs.

Brodie sighed. It was a damned nuisance being Saguaro Vista's most eligible male. Bachelorhood—however much he relished it—came complete with its own set of complications.

This woman, though, he decided as he drew closer to her, didn't look as though she had an immodest bone in her body. She also didn't look as though she'd whip out a purple marker and ask him to write 'To Trish, with love' on her left breast, as the redhead on his flight from Barbados had this morning.

But then . . . he considered the crazy idea he'd just come up with.

From behind him, Jennifer called out, "It's no good trying to sneak right back out without seeing her, Brodie. She's got *interviews* set up for the whole week."

He waved away her concerns. He wasn't the kind of guy who sneaked away—especially from his matchmaking mother, SupraTech's founder and CEO. However, he was the kind of guy who didn't go down without a fight. And in this instance, he'd need a sparring partner.

Someone exactly like the jumpy-looking female staring at him from the short end of the L-shaped sofa.

Brodie moved closer, still watching her. She stared at him, bewildered, and took a step back. Her legs bumped against the sofa, stopping her.

Automatically, he checked out her dowdy dress-for-success suit and practical pumps. Clearly, this wasn't a woman who took chances with her attire . . . or anything else.

He studied her timid face and practical chin-length haircut, and almost sighed aloud. Jeez, she looked like she'd make a run for it if he so much as smiled at her.

Brodie had to try anyway. If he didn't come up with something, he would be obliged to wine and dine the 'interview candidates' his mother had lined up for him. He'd have to make small talk with them all, pretend to be flattered by their interest in his family's famous company—and find a way to tell each of them nicely that the only one who wanted Brodie Richardson married was Nora Richardson, his overbearing mother.

For an instant, he paused, distracted by the jittery way the woman shoved her huge horn-rimmed glasses higher onto her nose. Maybe it wasn't that bad, Brodie thought in a panic. Maybe his mother hadn't even lined up that many women this time. Maybe . . .

He looked over his shoulder at Jennifer. As though she'd read his mind—which she probably had, given the number of times they'd been through this scenario—the receptionist held up nine fingers. She frowned, curled them in for an instant, and then raised all ten fingers.

Aaack. It was that bad.

Brodie turned back to the woman. "You're probably going to think this is nuts." It *was* nuts. He paused, shoved his hand through his hair and squinted, trying to decide how to phrase the impromptu proposal he had in mind. "But I really need your help."

"My help?"

Her voice was soft. Feminine. Sultrier than he'd expected. In surprise, Brodie angled his head to take a second look at her but all he saw was the same woman. With the same look. One that reminded him of the 'before' photos in the magazine makeovers his last girlfriend, Tara, had been so fond of. Plain, serious, and unsmiling.

"Yes, your help," he said, using the smile he'd heard his mother describe as charmingly boyish. "Okay?"

The woman blinked. She gazed over his shoulder—looking for a cue from Jennifer, he guessed—then looked into his face for the first time. He thought he glimpsed a defiant tightness in her lips, then dismissed the idea. She probably possessed about as much defiance as a plate of overcooked linguini.

"Actually . . ." She lowered her gaze to her sensible shoes as though they might morph into something sexy if she didn't keep a constant eye on them. "I don't think—"

"It'll only take a minute," Brodie interrupted. Suddenly, his initial impulse to come clean, explain to her about the blind-date-from-hell scheme his mother had cooked up, and then ask for her help didn't seem all that smart. He couldn't afford to waste time. And he couldn't risk having her bolt for the parking lot if she didn't want to play along. "Come on."

He reached for her arm. She flinched, a seemingly automatic gesture that made him frown in puzzlement. Slowing his movements a little, Brodie gave her a reassuring smile.

"You're here to see Mrs. Richardson, right?" he asked, noticing the death grip she maintained on her briefcase. Job interview jitters, if ever he'd seen them. Too bad she'd have to get her hopes crushed later. "For an interview?"

She looked at him suspiciously, then nodded. The action made reflected light sparkle in her dark hair and he liked the way it shone. Brodie caught himself wondering, foolishly, what her shampoo smelled like . . . and then realized, almost too late, what was going on.

The pressure was making him crack. And he'd only been back in town for one morning. Obviously, he couldn't take another round of matchmaking. Not even for the sake of his mother and the positive press it would engender for SupraTech's upcoming twenty-fifth anniversary celebration—his only reason for returning from the Caribbean at all.

"Well, then I'm the man you've got to see," he continued briskly, taking her arm in his. Startled all over again, the woman let herself be led a few steps toward the elevators while Brodie went on talking. He introduced himself to her—taking care to omit his surname. "I'll introduce you to her. Right this way."

Arm in arm, they neared the imposing oak door that guarded his mother's domain. Behind the door, a month's worth of dating nightmares waited for Brodie. Pausing to pull himself together, he looked down at his shy companion, and was struck with a ridiculous urge to smooth the crown of her shiny hair, and tell her everything was going to be all right.

He covered his unsettling impulse with a question. "What's your name?"

"Paige," she mumbled.

"Hmmm?"

"Paige," she said, a little louder this time. She stopped about a foot from the door, and darted a nervous glance at him. "Paige Mulvaney. It's all on my résumé. Here . . ."

She tried to tug her arm from his, obviously intent on wrestling her briefcase open and treating him to a read-through of her credentials. Brodie tightened his grasp to stop her, and was startled to feel the subtle pressure of her breast against his arm. A sudden vision of a white cotton bra, pert, perfect breasts, and a wildly inviting Paige blossomed in his brain.

Unnerved by the image, Brodie grabbed for the doorknob. What was the matter with him? He had to get this over with before he went completely crazy.

He jerked the door open. Beside him, Paige shrank back. Then she pulled in a deep breath—one Brodie felt every inch of, as her chest expanded against his bicep. She raised her chin. They were as ready as they were going to get.

Together, they stepped inside. Smiling, Brodie hugged Paige closer against him and faced the dozen or so women assembled inside the office. He caught a brief glimpse of his mother's face as she looked up from a stack of papers on her desk, registered the chill of the air conditioner she always kept precisely at sixty-eight frigid degrees, and felt his insides clench with irritation at being forced to take such drastic measures. Then he shot an adoring look at the woman beside him and made the announcement that he hoped would buy him a month's worth of peace and quiet.

"Mom, everyone . . ." Brodie waved his free arm, indicating the ten candidates assembled in the office as well as Pierce, his mother's administrative assistant. "I'd like you to meet Paige Mulvaney." A few seconds passed. Brodie waited, letting the anticipation build, then he squeezed Paige tighter. "My fiancée."

Two

It wasn't until Paige heard the office door click softly shut behind the last person to leave that she regained her senses. Freed from the horrified paralysis that had struck her the moment the big lummox beside her had made his announcement, she reared back, intent on escaping the nightmare that her great opportunity had become.

Brodie kept her pinned to his side, which gave her a disturbing familiarity with the strength of his biceps, the hard wall of his chest . . . and the aggravating width of his arrogant grin.

"That went well, don't you think?" he asked.

At his amazingly stupid question, frustration and fury welled inside her. She opened her mouth to yell, to swear, to tell this, this crazy man exactly what he could do with his interview-wrecking introduction and his fiancée story. Just why his intelligent hazel eyes were looking at her with such pleasure right now was a mystery. Wriggling harder against him to free herself, Paige drew in a breath and prepared to really let him have it.

All that emerged was a frustrated little squeak.

He had the nerve to actually laugh.

It was the last straw. Pulling back her free arm, Paige tested the weight of her briefcase, gave it a good wind-up, then walloped him with it, right smack in the middle of his lean middle.

Brodie released her and bent double, gasping for breath. His arm churned, as though he wanted to say something more but couldn't do it. It was probably just as well. More than likely, it would be another lie. Knowing that, she guessed she ought to take satisfaction in having fought back against someone so obviously without moral scruples. Paige hugged her briefcase against her chest and tried to gloat.

But the sight of him hunched over like that took most of the steam out of her self-righteous indignation. Cautiously, she edged closer.

"Are you all right?" she asked.

He wheezed. She could see his shoulders shake as he fought for breath, and it worried her. What if she'd really hurt him?

"I-I'm sorry. I guess I got a little carried away." With a tentative motion, she raised her hand. Her palm hovered a few inches away from his broad shoulder, close enough that Paige felt the heat rising from his body. Maybe just a little friendly pat, to show that she really meant her apology. . . .

At the last instant, she snatched her hand back. Just being hauled up unwillingly against him had made her brain grind to a stop. It had made her body tremble and her senses race with the unaccustomed thrill of being held, however briefly, in

MAN OF THE YEAR

a man's arms. What in the world would touching him on purpose accomplish?

She was afraid to find out. Instead, she peered at his still shaking shoulders and said, "You really shouldn't have done that, though. None of those other candidates even got to finish their interviews—" *Including me.* "—because they all got shooed out of here so quickly. What did you think—"

Brodie jerked up his hand, palm out, in a clear demand for quiet. Paige complied, watching with concern as he straightened again. Grimacing, he wiped tears from his eyes with the heels of his hands.

Oh, jeez. She'd actually made a grown man cry!

Guilt assailed her. Maybe he was a good-for-nothing liar, but that didn't give her the right to make him bawl in the middle of his mother's office.

His mother's office. The full importance of the situation hit her in a rush. She'd assaulted the son of SupraTech's CEO! She'd never get the position she wanted now, Paige realized. Not even if she somehow managed to secure another interview. She was doomed. And all because of one madcap moment of personal assertiveness.

She should have known better. Reckless, impulsive behavior just wasn't Paige Mulvaney's specialty.

"Thank God you didn't start lecturing me like that when everyone was still in here," Brodie managed to say between gasps. "They never would have bought the fiancée bit."

"They won't buy it anyway!"

"Oh, yes, they will. They already have."

Something in his voice made her look up at him. He stood a few feet away, in a cocksure stance she supposed was typical for him, with his unshaven face creased in a smile and his eyes filled with humor. He'd been *laughing* at her!

And she'd been gullible enough to believe she'd actually hurt him. Ha! He was probably as impervious to pain as he was to responsible, courteous behavior.

"Look at the way my mother made everyone leave," he pointed out, as though in proof of his assertion.

"You told her we wanted to be alone!"

"Don't we?" Brodie waggled his eyebrows at her in a suggestive fashion.

As *if* Paige was buying that.

"Hmmph." She yanked her skirt hem lower, just in case. Something about his presence made her uncomfortably aware of herself as a woman—a woman who was used to being ignored. Couldn't he see that about her? "Any female who wants to be alone with you ought to have her head examined—"

"Hey!"

"And her morals, too."

"Zing!" Remarkably, his grin widened. "Got me with that one, didn't you? Subtle, but right on target, given our situation."

He didn't seem bothered by that fact. But why should he? This was a man who'd fib to his own mother. Emboldened by her uncharacteristic comment, Paige quit hugging her briefcase to her chest and started walking toward the door. She had another interview to arrange. Maybe IntelliCorp would consider hiring her. It wasn't as prestigious as SupraTech, but what the heck.

"I'm impressed," Brodie went on. The nearness of his voice meant that he'd followed her across the luxurious private office. "I didn't realize you had that much spirit."

"Well, I do," she bluffed. "And I . . . I" Oh, damn. Why not just say what she really thought? She'd never see him again, anyway. "I don't appreciate having my interview wrecked by the likes of you. Good-bye."

She turned, ready to make a dramatic exit. The sound of his voice spoiled her momentum.

"Actually," he said in a rush, almost as though he didn't want her to leave, "it's not as bad as you think. It wasn't a real interview.

That stopped her. Paige lowered her hand, only inches from the doorknob, and turned to face him. She crossed the short distance separating them. "What?"

"It was a fake. One of many scheduled for this week, I presume." Suddenly, he looked gleeful. "Until now, that is. Now, thanks to you, they'll all be canceled."

Paige blinked. "You're not making sense."

He sighed. "My mother is matchmaking. Whenever I'm in town, she tries to fix me up. As in forever. She uses these open interviews to weed out the daughters-in-law from the nevers-in-law."

"By luring them in with pretend help-wanted ads? That's reprehensible!"

"It's motherly love." Shrugging, Brodie gazed out the office window at the overcast skies and rain-soaked desert landscape outside. "Usually, all the candidates are perfectly aware of what's going on."

She frowned. "I wasn't."

He peered at her. "Didn't you think it was strange that the position was unspecified? That no particular credentials were required?"

Actually, Paige hadn't looked much past the fact that her longed-for opportunity might have arrived, at the very company she most wanted to work for. Defensively, she said, "I thought there was probably a new product under development, hence the need for more staff. Unspecified staff, for a top-secret project."

Brodie wrinkled his brows. The open skepticism in his expression spurred her onward.

"Nora Richardson practically invented smart appliances," Paige continued. "She made millions marketing user-friendly designs to the technologically challenged. I guess she can set up interviews however she wants to, but—"

The sweep of the office door opening right beside her cut off Paige in mid-sentence. Before she could say another word about her admiration for SupraTech's revolutionary approach, she found herself hauled into Brodie's arms again.

MAN OF THE YEAR 27

"I love it when you talk technology to me," he murmured—and then he kissed her, right on the mouth.

She felt remarkably good, Brodie realized as his lips met hers. For a woman who wasn't particularly glamorous, Paige Mulvaney suddenly felt irresistible—and soft and curvy and feminine, in all the right places. Surprised by his discovery, he gently nudged her mouth open a little wider . . . and deepened the kiss.

After all, it was for the sake of his fiancée cover story.

Wasn't it?

Sure.

And the fact that Paige had suddenly aroused his curiosity as no woman had in years was irrelevant. At least that's what Brodie told himself as he lowered one hand to the small of her back and drew her nearer.

Paige gave a little cry of protest—easily muffled by Brodie's answering murmur—and then melted against him. For one long, impossible moment, he found himself lost in the heated glide of their mouths coming together, in the chest-to-thighs contact of their bodies leaning closer. She surrendered to him in a sweet, almost innocent way that suddenly seemed much more erotic than the direct maneuverings of his more sophisticated fans.

He could begin to like this. Really. Just to be

sure, Brodie cupped her cheek in his hand, tilted her face at a new angle, and went on exploring.

"Oh!" cried a voice Brodie recognized as his mother's. "Terribly sorry, dear."

Her appearance didn't faze him. In fact, he ignored it, for the most part.

Brodie sensed movement, heard his mother whisper something about retrieving crucial files from her desk. There was no mistaking the interest in her voice or the matchmaking antennae that practically quivered when Nora passed by.

As though in confirmation, she gave him an affectionate pat on his shoulder. "Carry on, son," his mother said. "We'll talk at dinner."

The door closed, and Brodie went right on kissing Paige. There was a delicate little spot just at the corner of her mouth that begged for a tiny lick . . . or maybe a nibble. *Mmmmm.*

Suddenly, the door swooshed open again. "Oh, and bring your fiancée," his mother added. "Surely you two lovebirds can break apart long enough to enjoy a welcome-home dinner at Guido's. See you at seven!"

With a breezy wave that Brodie glimpsed just as he ended the kiss, his mother closed the door again. He returned to reality with a jolt. Dinner! What was he going to do about dinner?

Obviously, he'd been in too much of a panic to think this plan through. Now that he had a 'fiancée,' his family would expect to see her. Regularly. At dinners and brunches and parties and, most likely, at all the SupraTech twenty-fifth anniversary events, too.

He was doomed, Brodie realized. And all because of one crazy moment of personal inventiveness.

How could that be? It wasn't as though he should have known better. Reckless, impulsive behavior was Brodie Richardson's specialty.

"Well." With a little wiggle, Paige stepped from his arms. She bent to retrieve her briefcase—dropped, he assumed, in the heat of passion—and then straightened. "Well," she went on, sounding uncomfortable, "now that that's over with, I guess I'll be going."

"Going?"

"Yes."

She sounded certain, but she looked almost reluctant. Behind her glasses, her brown eyes seemed distant and distracted. And despite its pursed shape, her mouth seemed to tremble slightly, almost as though Paige had been on the verge of blurting out some shocking revelation, and had stopped herself just in time.

What could it have been?

Nothing, Brodie told himself. The only thing shocking about a woman like her was the fact that she hadn't already slapped him silly for lunging at her like he had. That was what made her so perfect for this whole phony fiancée scheme. She was safe. With someone like Paige, he wouldn't be risking a real commitment. He wouldn't stand a chance of getting in over his head.

Which was all for the best, really. What sense would it make to leap out of the marriage mart and into a real relationship?

She interrupted his musings by clearing her throat. "Excuse me. You're blocking the doorway."

"Huh?" Brodie looked, and saw that he was. He stepped sideways, and watched her open the door. At the last instant, he regained his senses. "Wait!"

Paige jerked to a stop, hunching her shoulders defensively around her ears as though she feared he'd manhandle her again. It was an idea which had its merits, Brodie thought. Then he took another look at her and shook his head.

He was safe. She wasn't his type at all, which no fewer than three people in his mother's office had felt compelled to point out earlier, in none-too-subtle asides. Did everyone who knew him truly believe he was that shallow? Did they all really believe he couldn't be interested in a woman who wasn't blond, busty, and a centerfold candidate?

Evidently so. The idea rankled.

"You can't leave yet," he said, reaching to close the door before Paige could slip through. "We have things to discuss. Plans to make!"

"No, thank you." Primly, she stepped into the hallway.

Brodie grabbed her arm. "I need you!" he cried, his voice a hoarse whisper. "You've got to help me. I promised them a fiancée . . ." His frantic wave indicated his mother, the fake interview candidates, and the SupraTech employees at large in the hallway. He swallowed hard. ". . . and now I have to deliver one."

She raised her eyebrow—a movement, Brodie noticed, that gave her an intimidatingly intellectual appearance. For the first time, he wondered if he might have underestimated her. Could it be that demure little Paige knew something he didn't know?

Nah. "I have to have a fiancée. Tonight!"

"Hmmm." Paige studied the handle of her briefcase thoughtfully. "Ought to be no trouble for a guy like you."

"A guy like me?"

He could see the wheels turning in her mind. At the last moment, she appeared to think better of whatever she'd been about to say, and settled for, "One who's willing to take advantage of every possible . . . opportunity."

Suddenly, Brodie felt ashamed. Sorry for having used her to sidestep his dating dilemmas, and embarrassed that she'd seen through him so easily.

But then normalcy returned, and with it came his usual confidence. What did she know? Any other sought-after bachelor desperate for a little peace and quiet might have done exactly the same thing.

"Come on," he coaxed, flashing her the smile that had launched a thousand tabloid feature stories. "It'll be fun."

"For you, maybe," Paige murmured. "Not me. Good luck, Brodie."

And then the unthinkable happened.

She walked away from him, and straight out the front door.

Three

"I can't believe you didn't go for it."

Paige, barely awake and dressed in pajamas, stopped beside the gurgling coffeemaker in her kitchen and looked over her shoulder at her roommate. "Huh?"

"I can't believe you didn't go for it," April said again. She flipped her long red ringlets over her shoulder and twisted in her chair at the kitchen table to peer disbelievingly at Paige. "I would have. In a heartbeat."

"With Brodie, you mean?" Peeking upward to glimpse April's answering nod, Paige poured herself a cup of coffee and carried it to the table. She seated herself opposite her old friend, and shook her head. "I told you yesterday. It wasn't like that."

"Like what?"

"Like he actually wanted to go out with me." Embarrassed by the admission, Paige hunched her shoulders and gazed into her cup of coffee. Wisps of hazelnut-scented steam rose from its surface and curled in the air, sending her into a reverie. She tried, really tried, not to think about Brodie Richardson. She had a strong feeling that the passion she'd sensed in his kiss had been approximately as real as their 'engagement.'

Trouble was, she'd *wanted* to believe it.

She'd wanted to believe a man like him could really want a woman like her. Wanted to believe that someone had seen more in her than books and brains and theories. Wanted to believe, for one insane moment, that she'd been more than convenient and available.

Silly her.

"He didn't mean it," Paige explained, for what had to be the tenth time since coming home yesterday. "He was desperate, that's all."

"Are you kidding me?" Sitting crosslegged atop her straight-backed chair—a funky thrift store find she'd repainted—April laughed. She raised her arms and lowered her voice.

"Please," she begged in a false male voice, "please date me for a month. I know I'm the most sought-after bachelor in the southwest. I know I'm tall, dark and handsome, wealthy and famous, but please, can't you overlook all that and just go out with me? I'm begging here!"

Sighing, Paige waved away her roommate's antics and dragged over the briefcase she'd abandoned atop the table after coming home from yesterday's interview debacle. The last thing she wanted was to be reminded of Brodie's outrageous offer in the SupraTech parking lot afterward—and her own gullible reaction to it.

But April only dropped to her knees atop the linoleum. "Come on!" she pleaded in her deepest voice, knee-walking toward Paige's chair with her hands clasped at her chest. "I need you! I know I kiss like a dream and I—"

"I never said that!" Paige interrupted, laughing.

"You never had to." With a wink, April got back in her chair and crossed her legs again. "That stop-sign-red blush of yours says it all."

For an instant, Paige was whipped back into that moment, back into Brodie's strong arms and the wonder of his kiss. No one had ever kissed her like that before.

And, more than likely, no one would ever kiss her like that again, either. Sigh.

"It doesn't matter." She took a fortifying slurp of coffee, then admitted the truth. "He's not even very nice."

"But cute."

"And he's arrogant."

"But sexy.

A new blush heated Paige's face. "And according to you, he doesn't do anything but travel around, going to gala benefits and charity balls, getting photographed with a margarita in one hand and . . ."

"Sounds like fun." April winked.

". . . and a bimbo in the other."

April frowned and waved away the imaginary rival for Brodie's affections. "So what?" She selected a home-baked muffin from the wicker basket in the center of the table, and thoughtfully savored a bite. "It would be a good time. What have you got to lose?"

My heart, a tiny whisper inside Paige replied. But that didn't even make sense. And as a person who valued logic above all else, she couldn't start running around making decisions based on a hunch, or a premonition, or whatever this weird feeling was. She had to remain sensible.

And the sensible answer to Brodie's proposition had been no. It was still no. Pretending to be his fiancée for a month, as he'd asked, would be a bad idea—no matter what April said . . . and no matter how curious Paige might be.

She wondered if there would be more kisses involved.

"I'm not like Brodie," she told April. "I can't do things casually. I can't kiss someone and not feel anything afterward."

"So, what did you feel?" April asked. She offered Paige a mango muffin from the basket, and gave her a sassy grin to go along with it. "When he kissed you, I mean."

"I felt like I was a convenient distraction!" She scowled. "I felt like he wanted to throw his mother off the track, and I came in handy."

"Handy, huh?" April winked again. "Sounds promising."

"Arrgh! You're incorrigible."

"You know, you could get something out of this deal," April mused. "Live a little. Have some fun, before you settle into premature middle age with only your briefcase for company."

Paige smoothed a protective hand over her case's cracked leather. "What do you mean?"

"I mean, it would be a month's worth of dates with a gorgeous, eligible guy! Do you really think there's a downside to that?"

April didn't understand, Paige told herself. Even when she wasn't in the kitchen or on the job at the gourmet catering company she worked for, April was still cooking. Men fell for her like trees for a lumberjack. She didn't know what it was like to be overlooked.

"I don't know," she hedged. "I really ought to be lining up more job interviews."

"You really ought to be living a little! This is your big chance," April insisted. "Seize the day! Tell Brodie you want the deluxe treatment—flowers, candy, candlelit dinners, the works. You deserve something for helping him out of this jam."

You know, Paige realized as she finished her muffin and wadded up the paper liner, *I do, don't I?* Maybe she ought to . . .

Nah. It was impossible. She'd never work up the necessary nerve.

"I can't," she said with a shake of her head. "I won't."

Paige heard the thump of the newspaper being delivered at their apartment's front door, and got out of her chair to retrieve it. "I'm not going to pretend to be Brodie Richardson's fiancée, and that's that. I just want to forget the whole thing, and get back to my ordinary life."

She opened the front door. "There she is!" someone cried.

Dozens of flash attachments flared, brighter than

the early morning sunlight. Cameras whirred, and the babble of multiple frenzied voices echoed from the stuccoed walls of her apartment complex.

"Paige, over here!" yelled a photographer. In a daze, she stared at the reporters, news camera crews, and curious neighbors who thronged the usually quiet courtyard.

Yikes! Executing a jerky bend, Paige scooped up the newspaper. She turned, shutting the front door on the din outside, and hurled the paper toward the kitchen table.

"Oh my gosh!" she gasped, flattening her back against the closed door. "Did you see that?"

"Unbelievable!" April cried at the same time, whipping open the *Arizona Territorial*, staring at the front page. "Did you see this?"

They both looked. There, in black and white, was a large photo of Paige and Brodie, taken outside the SupraTech offices. They stood close, facing each other as though in deep negotiation—which they had been—over his outrageous proposition. The newspaper, however, had put a different, more romantic, spin on their tête-à-tête—and the headline screamed it for all to see:

Is It Love? Meet Brodie Richardson's Mystery Woman!

Paige gazed at the picture again. She traced her fingers over the photo, and knew that her safe, ordinary life would never be the same again. Darn that Brodie! He'd probably done this on purpose— leaked the story to the press in order to get her to agree to his scheme.

Well, if he thought he could wrap her around

his little finger that easily, Paige told herself, he'd better think twice.

A loud knock sounded at the door. She jumped, clutching the edges of her bathrobe in fright, and stared with wide eyes at April. "What are we supposed to do now?"

"I dunno." Her roommate strode to the door, looked through the peephole, and then gazed over her shoulder. As usual, she discovered a business angle to the whole mess. "But this could really give a jump to my baked-goods reputation. Do you think paparazzi like mango muffins?"

Brodie rounded the corner to Paige's apartment complex in his borrowed commercial van and spotted the news vehicle, double-parked reporters' cars, and curious onlookers. The press had beaten him there.

Couldn't they at least have given a guy a chance to finish his breakfast and get in some exercise before descending like wolves on his supposed 'mystery woman?'

Evidently not. Frowning, Brodie directed his companions toward a mostly deserted corner of the parking lot. Gesturing for one of the two men to join him, he hefted a roll of red shag from the back of the van and then watched as the other man did the same. Then Brodie tugged his borrowed carpet store uniform cap over his forehead, shouldered his unwieldy burden, and made his way through the crowds to apartment A-9.

Frantic feminine conversation greeted his knock. He couldn't make out the words from behind the closed door. A few seconds later, a voice he didn't recognize asked, "Who is it?"

"Delivery of your new double-plush shag, ma'am," he said. He touched the rim of his cap, just to make his story look good, and grinned at his companion. Kevin, an old friend from his Saguaro Vista High School days, had helped him out like this on more than one occasion. This was only the latest in a long line of fancy footwork and great escapes.

"The two rolls you ordered last month," Kevin put in, stifling a guffaw at Brodie's incognito routine. "With triple spot protection and a ten year guarantee."

More muffled consultation. There was a scraping sound, then a bump. Sobering his grin, Brodie raised his face to the door's peephole and puckered his lips. He blew a kiss.

The door opened a crack. He glimpsed Paige's face, pale beneath her mussed dark hair. Behind her stood a redhead, her hand firm on the door to keep it from opening further as she demanded, "But how do you know it's him?"

"I just do, that's all." Blushing, Paige opened the door wide enough that he and Kevin could slip inside with their matching rolled-carpet burdens. "Hello, Brodie."

Brodie propped his roll against the wall. He smiled. "She's familiar with these lips," he explained, giving both women another teasing pucker. "Don't you read the papers?"

"Don't you know when to quit?" Paige shut the door against the renewed baying of the newshounds, then locked it. Folding her arms across her chest, she glared at him with all the grandeur of a princess in pajamas. "I already told you, I'm not helping you. So what are you doing here?"

"I came to rescue you. Of course."

"Ha!"

"Really." He moved nearer to her, passing the redhead . . . who seemed to have taken a fancy to Kevin, and was absorbed in a flirty discussion about the excellent fit of his uniform. Brodie looked up and down at Paige's pink fuzzy slippers, plaid bathrobe, and flower-print pajamas.

His gaze centered on the pajama top's button placket. Brodie experienced a dizzying urge to undo the top button, and find out if her skin felt half as soft as it looked. Instead, he frowned and said, "You'll need to change clothes first, of course."

"What for?"

"For escaping the reporters." He gave her a little smack on the derrière to hurry her along, and was delighted to discover how nice and soft and curvy Paige felt. "Let's go. I have to have the carpet van back by lunchtime."

Instead of complying, as he'd expected, Paige blushed more deeply and stood her ground. "What if I don't want to go?"

"Don't be ridiculous." Jeez, she was showing a

remarkable lack of gratitude for his heroism. Especially considering the fact that Brodie had hauled himself away from his safe haven solely for the sake of tracking her down and helping her out of what had to be a bizarre situation for her. "Would you rather wrangle with the reporters outside? They won't leave, you know. Not as long as they smell a story."

"Well, well . . ." She waved her hand in the air, looking as though her modest apartment might magically offer up some solution. "Maybe I'll just give them a story. Maybe I'll just go outside and tell them the truth."

"About us?" He gulped.

She nodded.

"You're bluffing."

"Want to try me?"

Brodie considered. "Sure."

He grabbed her by the arm, unlocked the door with one hand, and opened it wide, keeping himself hidden behind it. Silhouetted in the opening by the brilliant light of flash cameras, Paige froze. "I changed my mind!" she yelped.

"I thought so." Brodie got them both back inside and closed the door again before they provided the Saguaro Vista press with a month's worth of juicy 'love nest' photos. "Let's go."

Her face took on surprising stubbornness. "I'm not leaving without April. You've got to help her, too."

"Your roommate?" Brodie motioned to the redhead, who was feeding bites of mango muffin to an appreciative Kevin. "I have to admire your loyalty, but I think she's going wherever Kevin's going."

"And that's with you?"

"Yup."

"How?" She raised her eyebrow in the infuriatingly brainy gesture he was already coming to associate with her. "We can't exactly march out there and expect to avoid the reporters."

"Leave it all up to me," Brodie said, watching as Paige disappeared down a short hallway and into what he assumed was her bedroom. "I've got it all planned out."

"That's what I was afraid of," she yelled. She shut her door to change clothes.

Brodie Richardson drove about as carefully as he selected kissing partners, Paige decided as she listened to the tires of his shiny red Mercedes convertible squeal around a corner. They sped through the desert landscape, brightened now with green-leafed mesquite and early summer wildflowers. The pungent tang of damp creosote bushes sharpened the air, mingling with the smell of the luxury car's leather seats and the faint scent of new carpet that still clung to Brodie's borrowed uniform. They were driving to a place Brodie had assured her would be free of reporters. Paige just hoped they'd get there in one piece.

"You know," he said, shifting his gaze from the stretch of road outside Saguaro Vista to her face for one terrifying, overlong instant, "your head won't blow away if you quit holding on to it."

"Maybe not," she shouted to be heard over the wind blowing inside the convertible. "But my hairstyle will!"

"So what?" Brodie shrugged. "I'm the only one who'll be seeing it. Go ahead. Live a little."

His smile suggested she'd look terrific all tousled and windblown—regardless of the frowzy hairdo sure to result. No woman could resist such by a smile. And Paige didn't. With a small shiver of recklessness, she lowered her hands from her ears.

"There you go!" he said, nodding encouragingly.

Wind rushed through her hair, making the ends toss around her face. Through the rapidly tangling brown strands, she glimpsed Brodie's expression of pleasure, and grew bold enough to actually toss her head. She was Grace Kelly in *To Catch A Thief*. She was Audrey Hepburn in *Breakfast At Tiffany's*, minus the chic scarf and sunglasses. She was Julia Roberts in anything. She was . . . forced to scrape a big hank of Chapstick-coated hair out of her mouth when an especially gusty breeze blew across the car.

How come that never happened in the movies?

Brodie laughed and scrabbled around one-handed behind the driver's seat. He came up with a baseball cap and tossed it to her. "Maybe this will help."

"Thanks." She tugged it on, feeling ridiculous—and about as glamorous as a sandlot pitcher. Sinking as low in the cushy seat as her seat belt would allow, Paige gazed morosely at the rock formations beside the road. "Where are we going, anyway?"

They'd dropped off April at the catering company, and had left Kevin with the van and the lone carpet company employee who'd accompanied their great escape. Being rolled up in several yards of bordello-red shag and carried over Brodie's shoulder to the back of the van hadn't been fun, but Paige had to admit, it had been effective. They'd managed to elude the press and get out of town without being spotted. The question now was . . . what next?

"We're going to my secret hideaway," Brodie said. His grin made her imagine a super spy bachelor pad, with mirrors over the bed, a paneled bar, and lots of chrome and leather furniture. "Usually, I'd just issue a statement and go on with my usual plans, but now that you're involved, it only seemed fair to give you a chance to adjust before making any big decisions for the two of us."

His thoughtfulness surprised her. "Thanks. I have to admit, it was a little jarring to find reporters camped out beside my potted petunias and the hibachi grill."

"I'll bet. You're handling it great, though."

He squeezed her hand, then returned his grasp to the steering wheel. For a moment, Paige watched him drive, mesmerized by the strong, masculine shape of his hands, by the decisive movements he made . . . by the fact that he'd touched her, with no ulterior motive beyond good will.

Maybe Brodie wasn't such a bad guy, after all.

If the past two days were any indication, he probably spent a significant portion of his life hounded by reporters and camera people. It couldn't be an easy existence. Yet he handled it all with good cheer, and was obviously interested in helping her do the same. Maybe she should reevaluate her opinion of him.

"And besides," he continued blithely, "it will only be for a month or so. Once our 'engagement' is officially off, the press will leave you alone. Don't worry."

Her reevaluation ground to a halt. "You make it sound as though I've agreed to that ridiculous fiancée scheme of yours."

"Haven't you?"

"No!" Paige's formerly charitable thoughts vanished. "No! Of course not!"

"Why not?"

"Well. It's a lie, for starters."

"So is the modest little educational summary on the résumé you left at SupraTech yesterday," Brodie pointed out. "But that didn't stop you. You have three degrees, not two."

"My economics degree wasn't relevant to the SupraTech position," she hedged. "Besides, I—"

"And," he continued doggedly, "you were the youngest recipient ever of the Lancaster Award for Saguaro Vista youth. In addition to which, you possess not one, not two, not three, but six patents for various home technology inventions." He slowed at a street sign, then turned right and accelerated again.

Paige couldn't hold back a self-conscious grin. "Guilty as charged," she admitted, pushing up her eyeglasses.

"I'm an inventive woman." Telling people about her various accomplishments ofter made them look at her as if she were some kind of freak—an IQ on parade. For some reason, she wanted Brodie to see her as something more.

Paige went on. "But that's not important. We're talking about you and your fiancée fix, not me. You'll just have to find someone else."

"I want you," he said stubbornly.

How she wished that were true, all of a sudden! Dispirited, Paige folded her hands in her lap and stared down at the checked shirt and ratty blue jeans she'd grabbed in a rush from her closet this morning. Then she uttered the words she'd never expected to find herself saying to any man—much less one as gorgeous as Brodie. "Well. You can't have me."

"Why not?" Brodie asked again. "Afraid to have some fun?" He parked the car in front of a modest southwestern-style house. "Afraid to seize the day?"

Seize the day. It was exactly what April had said. The words tugged at her, urging her toward something Paige felt sure she would regret in the cold light of tomorrow—or sooner.

She resisted. "I'm not afraid of anything."

"Oh, no?" Brodie unfastened his seat belt, a movement that revealed the tight white T-shirt beneath his uniform—and the impressive muscles that caused it to be tight in the first place. With a knowing smile, he leaned sideways and unbuckled Paige's belt for her. Slowly, he eased the fastener across her middle and let it snap back just over her shoulder. His knuckles grazed her cheek. "Then why do you jump every time I touch you?"

"Ummm, I . . ." Her heart skittered into a faster rhythm. She gathered her rapidly unraveling thoughts and tried to ignore the subtle caress of his fingers against her skin. "I . . ."

"You're afraid of me, Paige. That's what you're afraid of."

Silently, she shook her head. However much she wanted to, she couldn't muster a more coherent protest. Who'd have thought that the touch of a man's hand against a body part so innocuous as her cheek could have such an effect on her?

"You're afraid of what I might make you feel," Brodie continued, his voice a seductive rasp that heightened her senses almost as much as his touch did.

Paige shivered beneath the tumultuous consequences of both. "I'm not afraid of you," she managed to say.

"You're bluffing."

"I am not!"

A devilish grin preceded his next remark by the space of a breath. "Prove it."

"Okay." Paige said simply. "I'll be your fiancée for a month. That's how unafraid I am of you."

Her sense of triumph was short-lived. "Super," Brodie said. He leaned away and pulled the keys from the ignition, then got out and came around to her side to open the door. As he did, he grinned again, just as though he'd known the outcome of their conversation all along.

And maybe he had.

The idea rankled.

"But only on one condition," Paige blurted out.

"Hmmm?" Brodie paused, one hand on the roadster's door handle. "What's that?"

"I want the works," she said. "The whole dating enchilada—candles, candy, flowers—"

"Jewelry?" His expression said he was teasing her.

"Sure!" she cried recklessly. She was on a roll now. "Everything a real fiancée would get." *Except love,* she thought, wincing. Paige ignored her heart. "I want to feel like the most sought-after woman on the planet, or the deal's off. Got it?"

"Sure." Brodie shrugged. "Is that all?"

Despite his casually voiced question, he seemed concerned. Hesitant, almost. Was he having second thoughts about their arrangement?

And if he was, why did Paige suddenly feel so bereft? It was what she should have wanted. Rescue from her own recklessness.

"Yes. That's it," she said cautiously.

"Great." He opened the door and offered his hand to help her out of the car. "Come on inside, and we'll get started."

Feeling her body quiver with nervousness, Paige stepped out and followed him up the walk. Brodie's hand guided her from behind, resting lightly on the small of her back as he maneuvered them both toward the front door. On an impulse, he slipped his palm lower, then cupped her derriere for the barest fraction of an instant. His sound of appreciation unnerved her almost as much as his bold touch did.

At the door, Brodie ducked his head and sorted through his keys. "We have a lot of catching up to do," he remarked, selecting the appropriate key and fitting it into the lock. "I generally make love to my fiancées before getting engaged to them."

Four

Brodie knew he was going to pay for that crack about sleeping with his fiancées.

But it was worth it, to ease the unaccustomed edginess he felt in bringing Paige to the house he never shared with any of his mother's matrimonial picks. And it was worth it, too, to see Paige's lips part in surprise, and to hear the faint gasp she gave as he pushed open the front door and showed her inside.

Nervously, she edged past him, whisking off her baseball cap as soon as the door closed against the rain-scented June breeze. In the light from the foyer windows, her hair shone like caramel and honey, making him want nothing more than to smooth the strands away from her blushing cheeks.

Who'd have guessed that mousy little Paige could have looked so . . . well, almost cute . . . while shocked to the toes of her clunky sneakers?

It was enough to make Brodie want to shock her all over again.

And since he wasn't the kind of guy to sidestep a rewarding impulse, however outrageous, he did.

"We're in luck, too," he told her, walking past

her into the living room. "I don't think we're expected anyplace until dinner tonight—my mother was really disappointed to hear that we had to reschedule at Guido's last night, by the way—so we have all the time in the world."

"T-time?"

"To get to know one another." Brodie gave her a suggestive grin. He just couldn't help himself. "Thoroughly."

"Uhhh . . ."

"Slowly."

"Ummmm . . ."

"Pleasurably." He drew out the word, lengthening it into an anticipatory growl. "Just the two of us."

"I-I see."

To give her credit, Paige looked game enough—if he discounted the astonished look her eyes had taken on behind her horn rims, and the way her sneakers seemed to be glued to the foyer tiles. Maybe she'd be able to play along with this fake fiancée scheme, after all.

"So we'd better get started," he said. "Don't you think so?"

She goggled. Brodie smiled. He unbuttoned his uniform shirt and shrugged it off, then casually tossed it toward the sofa with his best bachelor's free-throw aim. The shirt sailed toward its target, passing by the end table and drawing Brodie's attention to the four statuettes arranged there. Damn! In his haste to get started on his plan, he'd forgotten to stow the humanitarian award, the fellowship award, the good neighbor award, and the eco-awareness award in some safe place until this was over with. Brodie put his hands to his T-shirt and began pulling it over his middle.

Another gasp from Paige stilled his hands. Curiously, he lowered his arms far enough to peek through them, and was rewarded with the sight of Paige standing a few feet away, gawking openly at his muscular abdomen.

Well, well. With womanly appreciation like that for an incentive, he'd add more reps the next time he hit the gym. Grinning to himself, Brodie took his time in peeling off his T-shirt, then flung it atop the telltale awards.

By the time he looked up again, Paige had regained her attitude. She peered at him through her eyeglasses and asked, "Is everyone in your family as genetically gifted as you?"

Despite his resolve not to, Brodie preened. Sure, a guy didn't want to be valued for his physique alone, but . . .

"Could be." He shrugged and attempted to look modest. "I can't speak for anyone else, but—"

"Statistically speaking, they probably are," she concluded. She propped her chin against her upraised hand and studied him. "It's too bad things got dished out so disproportionately. It must be tough for you, knowing that your parents' intellectual capabilities were passed on to one of your siblings, while you . . . well, you simply got stuck with brawn."

This time, it was Brodie's turn to boggle. "Stuck with brawn? Did you actually say *stuck* with—"

"There's no need to feel bad about it," Paige muttered, quickly on the defensive. "We all have our individual attributes. Obviously, the adjective 'babelicious' doesn't describe me."

With a slight scowl, she fingered the untucked shirttails of her shirt and sighed. *"Really* obviously."

Brodie shook his head. "Now there," he said, "is where you're wrong."

"But I'm quite good at other things," she continued cheerily, as though he hadn't spoken. She resettled her eyeglasses on the bridge of her nose. "For instance, I'm a whiz at standardized tests. And I aced April at every ping-pong match we ever held. And I've never met a computer I didn't like."

He couldn't stand it. Brodie certainly didn't consider himself as insensitive as she made him out to be. And he definitely wasn't the kind of guy who backed out on an agreement.

"Babeliciousness," he said, moving closer to her, "is in the eye of the beholder."

"Yeah, right."

"And I"—Brodie brought his hands to her shoulders, and felt her tremble at the contact—"am developing a certain appreciation for what I'm beholding right now."

Paige rolled her eyes. "Come on, Brodie. I know perfectly well what I look like."

"Hmmm-mmm." The realization that she did not, could not, struck him all at once. "I don't think you do."

"Look, I don't want our deal to extend to lying. Okay? Let's just get that clear, right up front."

"Okay." Slowly, he slid his palms over her shoulders, moving toward the primly buttoned collar of her shirt. "But, I'm not lying when I say I like touching you. Or when I say how much I've been wanting to do this."

Brodie unfastened her topmost button, baring a tantalizing triangle of creamy skin, and releasing the combined scents of soap and lemony perfume. Inhaling appreciatively, he lowered his fingers to the next button. He twisted it gently . . .

Paige's hand clamped over his. "Don't insult us both by resorting to games. As long as I'm a female with a pulse, you're willing to get me naked. Admit it."

He shrugged. "I admit it."

The ah-hah! he sensed would come next never did. Instead, she only loosened her grasp on his hand. "At least you're capable of honesty."

"I'm capable of a lot more than that. Let me show you."

Her eyebrow rose in that skeptical quirk that seemed suddenly, uniquely Paige's. "Show me what?"

"That however eager I might be to get a woman naked"—Brodie ducked his head, hoping to hide the ridiculous hopefulness that rose within him—"it's not something I do casually." He lifted his gaze to her face, looking deeply into her eyes. Were those tears he glimpsed there? He hoped not.

"Oh, Brodie. I almost believe you mean that."

The huskiness in her voice spurred him on. "I do," he said, and unfastened another button, letting his fingers linger over the upward swell of her breasts. A fierce curiosity urged him to look down at the gentle curves he'd partially revealed.

Brodie resisted. He gazed into Paige's misty brown eyes instead, and told her what he felt. "Your skin," he said truthfully, "feels like silk against my hand. Warm and smooth and so soft that I could go on touching you for days, and still not get enough."

Paige's mouth dropped open. Then she recovered. "It's the lipid action of my lemon balm body lotion," she said quickly. "It traps the moisture inside the—"

"Shhh." He fought back the grin that rose to his lips, thinking that he'd never met anyone like Paige Mulvaney before. "Don't think. Just . . . feel."

After a confused wrinkling of her brow, she complied. With a sigh, Paige closed her eyes and tilted her head back. She pursed her lips, as though trying to recall the answer to a trick question.

"Not so hard," Brodie urged. "Just relax."

She sighed, and her body eased beneath his hands. Satisfied, he went on exploring. He nudged open the next button on her shirt. Since Paige's eyes were closed, Brodie felt free to look his fill.

Then Brodie experienced the last emotion he'd expected to feel. It wasn't lust, quite, although the small curves of her breasts, just barely visible under the folds of green-checked fabric, did inspire some of that. And it wasn't love—he could never fake that.

It was something even more unusual. He looked again at Paige's trusting, expectant posture before Brodie recognized his feeling for what it was.

Tenderness.

It couldn't have been easy, he realized in that moment, for a woman like Paige to reveal herself to him. To embrace the kooky plan he'd concocted, and put herself at risk to help him.

He would never, Brodie swore silently, give her a reason to doubt her decision. No matter what happened, he would not allow Paige to be hurt because of him.

"What do you feel?" he whispered.

She cracked open one eye. "I feel . . . silly."

Shoving the baseball cap beneath her elbow, she seized the edges of her shirt and rapidly rebuttoned it, until only the topmost button remained undone.

He noticed the speedy movements of her fingers, and put on a sorrowful face. "Does this mean we won't be getting to know one another better?"

"Better. Not intimately."

"Spoilsport."

"I'm not a spoilsport. I just like to do things efficiently." Paige assumed a businesslike air, and surveyed the room. "In this case, efficiency means I get to know what you like, and where you spend your time."

Brodie imagined his home as seen through her eyes—glossy wood floors, overstuffed Navajopatterned sofa, gigantic home theater system with video game controllers snaking a path from the electronics system to the middle of the floor—and battled an urge to grab back his T-shirt. Standing there, with her, he felt suddenly vulnerable.

Maybe this plan wasn't such a brilliant idea, after all.

She walked further into the room, running her fingertips dangerously close to the T-shirt-shrouded award statuettes on the end table. "Do you live here alone?"

He nodded. "This was a prototype house which was hardwired for some of SupraTech's early smart appliances. After my mother was finished with it, I bought it and moved in. My official address is a condo in town, but I'm never there for long."

"So I imagine. Especially with the press hounding you the way they do."

"We're safe here," he assured her. "Nobody knows about this place."

"Nobody except me and about a dozen other former 'fiancées,' I suppose." Paige pursed her lips, then strode through the archway to the dining room. There, she examined the newspaper-strewn tabletop with curious intensity. "Do you acquire a new fiancée every time you come back to Saguaro Vista?"

Brodie frowned. It was official, he realized. His carefree playboy cover had worked so well that everyone around him believed it. So why wasn't he happier about it?

And why couldn't a smart girl like Paige see through it?

"Every other time," he joked. "A guy's got to take some time off from phony engagements every once in a while."

Paige nodded in mock commiseration. "Of course."

"What about you?" Brodie asked. "Is there some guy waiting in the wings for you, once this is all over with?"

"Mmmm." Thoughtfully, she turned the baseball cap round and round in her fingers, staring at the brim as though it might hold the answer to his question. "Not at the moment," she finally said.

Brodie released a breath he hadn't been aware of holding. Geez, a person would think he cared whether or not Paige Mulvaney had a boyfriend. When, of course, that couldn't be the case.

"Good." He moved nearer, mindful of his promise to make her feel like—what was it she'd said?—the most sought-after woman on the planet. Gently, Brodie removed the baseball cap from her hand and flung it onto the dining room table beside them. He took both her hands in his, then smiled. "That will make doing this much easier."

And with no more warning than that, he lowered his head and kissed her.

"Mmmph!" Doing her best to wriggle away from the sudden—and sensually compelling—descent of his lips on hers, Paige tried to twist her head to the side, out of reach. Instead, she only managed to move her mouth closer to Brodie's. Of their own accord, her hands tightened in his, and the subtle rasp of his big, masculine palms against hers suddenly seemed the most exciting sensation ever, second only to his kiss.

This wasn't the best way to get to know one another. They needed a plan. A strategy. A conversation.

But aside from that fact, it seemed her body had already bought into this phony fiancée business. Hook, line, and sinker. Sinking . . . sinking . . . with no more conscious thought than that, Paige found herself melting into Brodie's warm embrace, feeling his body press against hers, pushing them both against one of the high-backed chairs surrounding the dining-room table.

His thumbs rubbed over the backs of her hands, the only steadying influence in a world suddenly gone hot and dizzying. He kissed her as if he couldn't wait another minute to taste her, as if he'd been dying to feel their lips slide together this way, slow and wild and wonderful. With a low groan, Brodie urged her to open her mouth still wider, and Paige willingly did. Her reward was a deepening of their kiss—and the incredible feeling that the big, strong man before her was helpless to resist her.

Oh, no. If she wasn't careful, she might actually fall for him. April had said to go for the works, not to get her heart stomped on. Reluctantly, Paige pulled her hands from Brodie's.

At her movement, he ended the kiss. When she dared to look up at him, he was gazing at her with a quizzical frown. "What's the matter?"

"We've already tried out our kissing routine," Paige said, giving him a shaky laugh. "Back at Supra-Tech, remember?"

"That was just the beginning."

"I think we've got it nailed. Two thumbs up."

"I think we need more practice." With a wicked smile, he reached for her again, evidently intent on proving it.

Paige sidestepped his grasp. He sighed in disappointment, a seemingly spontaneous response she almost believed. Brodie was good, she'd give him that. It would be easy, too easy, to believe he really wanted her. Already. What more practical magic would a few more weeks of physical proximity create?

Just in case, she mustered her defenses and went on. "And it will be the end, too, if we don't sit down for some serious conversation and get our stories straight before tonight."

"It's dinner at Guido's, not an inquisition."

"That's what you think." Determinedly, Paige edged her way past him, closing her eyes in an effort to resist the appealing sight of his broad, finely muscled chest a few inches from her nose—and then stepped toward the kitchen at the other end of the living space. "If anybody's going to believe that you and I are engaged, then we need to have to put in some serious study time."

He made a face. "Studying has never been my favorite activity."

"I didn't think so. Otherwise, you'd be—"

She stopped herself, about to say, *you'd be working in your family's company, instead of jet-setting all over the world.* Instead, Paige bit her lip at the hurt she saw flash over Brodie's face, and ended up with a lame-sounding, "—you'd be some other guy altogether, which you're not."

"No. I'm not."

He seemed to be waiting for her to apologize. Well, Paige decided defiantly, she wouldn't. After all, Brodie hadn't exactly fallen all over himself to deny *his* less-than-stellar opinions of her attractiveness. Now, had he?

No.

But the slow, sure progress of his fingers down her shirt buttons earlier—and the fascinated expression on his face at the time—could have managed to stand in nicely for an apology. If she'd believed he was sincere, which she hadn't, not for a second.

No matter how convincing he'd seemed.

Paige looked up again to find Brodie beside her with crossed arms and a fresh, tremendously cocky smile spreading across his face. What now?

"The well-developed among us," he pointed out, flexing his biceps, "are not necessarily the morons you think we are, you know. There may be more to me, Miss Smarty Pants, than a hot body."

"Sure. Whatever."

"And a killer grin." His widening of that grin said he was teasing now.

"I'm sure."

"And a habit of choosing the most attractive women to spend time with," Brodie continued. He cocked his head at a thoughtful angle. "Have I told you how much I like your eyes? They're a beautiful shade of brown."

Paige snorted.

"And I'm growing fond of your lips, too. I just had to get a little closer to see the truth."

Oh, boy. "Can't you do anything without turning it into an opportunity for a kiss?"

He appeared to think about it for a minute. "I'm not sure. I've never had to try."

She couldn't help but laugh. More than likely, he was right.

"But I do know this much," Brodie went on. "If we're not physically comfortable with each other—"

"Physically?" She gulped.

He nodded. "—tonight at dinner, then the jig is up. My family will never believe you're my fiancée if you edge sideways at my every touch."

"Hey! That's not a very flattering way to talk about the way I walk."

"And if you look ready to jump out of your skin whenever I look at you."

Guilty as charged. Paige lowered her eyes.

Brodie got to the point. "So loosen up."

He flicked his fingertip over the button placket of her shirt, pointedly touching the buttons she'd refastened nearly up to her chin. Paige swatted his hand away.

"*I* decide when, where and if I 'loosen up.' "

"Fine. And I'll 'share' as much information about my personal life as *I* decide."

"Fine."

"Fine."

"Good." With an emphatic nod, Paige ended their exchange. Strangely enough, she felt invigorated by sparring with him and thrilled to have asserted herself at last, however much Brodie scrambled her thoughts and set her inexperienced body to tingling whenever he came near. "Then let's get started," she said.

At Brodie's good-natured agreement, she turned to follow him into the kitchen where he promised to assemble sandwiches and drinks for their first getting-to-know-you session. And on the way there, with a devilish feeling simmering inside her, Paige reached up to her button placket again.

And unfastened the first two buttons.

Five

He'd lost his fiancée. Again.

This was getting to be a habit. One Brodie couldn't wait to break. Frowning, he looked up from the table for eight his mother had commandeered at Guido's and squinted toward the alcove that housed the ladies' room. Paige had escaped in that direction to 'freshen up' shortly after the appetizers had arrived at their table. By now, she'd had time to freshen up, jog around the block, and patent another of her brainy new inventions. Where was she?

The possibility that he was being jilted edged uncomfortably into his mind. In the movies, desperate women escaping dreadful dates typically ducked out a rest-room window and hightailed it toward the other end of town, leaving their hapless victims looking like fools.

Just like him.

Horrified at the possibility, Brodie jumped to his feet. At the motion, wineglasses wobbled, sending burgundy-colored flashes of light across the surprised faces of his parents, his brother and sister-in-law, and his cousin Jules, with her latest stockbroker conquest.

"Is something wrong?" Nora Richardson asked.

"Wrong?" Brodie choked out a laugh and gave an offhanded wave—one that nearly toppled the plate of calamari, stuffed mushrooms, and bruschetta in the center of the table. "What could be wrong?"

"I don't know." His mother gave him a pointed look, and dabbed at her lips with a napkin. She smoothed it over her lap. "That's why I asked."

"Nothing's wrong. I just need to talk to Paige for a minute. I'll be right back."

He tossed down his napkin and headed with what he hoped was a casual stride toward the ladies' room. Brodie realized that he was walking fast enough to make his pants legs flap, but by now he was too far gone to care.

"Isn't that cute?" His sister-in-law Shelby's voice drifted after him, filled with feminine assurance. "He can't bear to be separated from his new fiancée for a minute, can he?"

His traitorous family's murmured agreement was swallowed up by the sounds of other diners talking, flatware clinking against plates, and the low classical music that underlaid it all, just as Brodie reached the alcove. He rounded the archway, then stopped dead at the sight that greeted him.

Paige stood there, cradling the pay phone receiver to her ear. The recessed lighting above her cast beams of gold onto her dark hair as, with a curiously intimate gesture, she cradled the receiver nearer . . . and laughed.

Something uncharitable twisted in Brodie's gut. Paige hadn't fallen and broken a leg on a puddle of spilled hand soap. She hadn't been stricken with a sudden and mysterious illness, or given in to an irresistible urge to floss, or any of the other half-dozen things Brodie had imagined on his trek from the table to here. Instead, while he'd been sweating it out at their table, she'd been having a cozy tête-à-tête on the phone—probably with the boyfriend she claimed not to have.

What nerve.

And what a moron he was to care. Even a little.

A restaurant employee carrying a basket of long-stemmed red roses passed by the alcove, counting the tips she'd made selling the flowers to customers. Seized by an uncharacteristically practical impulse, Brodie caught her attention and started negotiating.

Paige finally spotted him just as he completed the deal. Her face paled. With a whispered goodbye to lover boy, she hung up the phone.

"Uh, hi," she said. Her folded arms made her long dress hike up a little. Now it nearly bared all of her calves. He'd definitely have to get her into somewhat more revealing attire. "I didn't know you'd come looking for me. Sorry."

"It's all right." Brodie completed his transaction with the flower seller, tucking two red roses beneath his arm while he paid up. "I needed to walk off some of that artichoke dip, anyway."

He patted his middle, as though calories were something he considered on a regular basis. Judging by her expression, Paige wasn't buying it.

"Brodie, I have to talk to you. It's about the dinner—" She broke off suddenly. Her gaze darted to the two red roses beneath his arm, and her face took on a dreamy quality. "Oh, no. Why did you get me flowers?"

"Oh, these?" Brandishing the two roses, Brodie raised his eyebrows. "They're not for you."

"They're not?"

"No."

"Oh. I just thought, well . . ." Paige wrapped her arms more securely around herself, and gave him a wobbly smile. "That's okay. A misunderstanding. I get it. Could've happened to anyone."

She sucked in a deep breath, and then she gestured toward the pay phone. "That was April. Those photographers outside the restaurant tonight really got to me, I guess. I called her for a little moral support."

Yeah, right, Brodie thought. *And I read the Sports Illustrated swimsuit issue for insights on the weather in Antigua and the Bahamas.*

Pushing aside his doubts about Paige and her mystery phone companion, he turned to the flower seller and accepted the two dozen red roses he'd paid for from her basket, then handed over the two he'd agreed to let her keep in order to finish out her shift. Brodie held the fragrant bundle toward Paige.

"*These* are for you," he said.

"Oh, Brodie!" Her eyes widened, and she stared with disbelief at the mass of flowers. "You didn't."

"I did."

"No."

"Yes."

She shook her head. "I thought the box of chocolates you surprised me with after I bought this dress was nice. But this . . ." Her eyes misted. "Well, you might as well know. I'm just not used to big romantic gestures."

"Then you're way overdue." Moving closer, Brodie offered her the roses. Paige continued to gape in disbelief. He wondered if she was going to leave him holding the gigantic bouquet, like some kind of lovesick goon, while the whole restaurant stared. His original indignation began to give way to a new feeling.

A new, mushy, I-hope-she-likes-them feeling.

It was a new experience for Brodie, and not a wholly comfortable one. Paige was bright, highly educated, and sensible. She wasn't likely to fall head over heels for a guy whose main claim to fame was . . . well, fame. Along with a passable face, a crooked smile, and more passport stamps than long-lasting relationships to his credit.

In short, she wasn't likely to fall head over heels for *him*, a fact that, until now, hadn't bothered him very much. But just at the moment, with Paige's sparkling brown eyes gazing at that armload of flowers with something curiously close to wonder, it began to matter very much, indeed.

Suddenly, Brodie wanted Paige. For himself. For

real. And he couldn't stand to think that she might not want him back. At least temporarily.

"My whole family is watching from across the restaurant," he lied, bending near enough to catch the scent of her perfume. "If you don't take these roses, they'll think something is wrong."

Biting her lip, Paige reached for the roses. Breathing a sigh that he refused to believe was a sigh of relief, Brodie watched as she buried her face in their dew-spangled red softness and inhaled deeply. Her eyes fluttered closed, and a rising blush colored her cheeks. Caught up in the pleasure of receiving the most romantic gift of all, bashful Paige Mulvaney seemed . . . well, almost beautiful.

"Thank you," she whispered.

Then she reached for the sleeve of his navy knit shirt, twisted her fingers in the fabric, and yanked him forcibly behind the cover of the alcove wall. Brodie stumbled after her in surprise, unbalanced by the strength of the pull.

She blinked, watching him straighten. "Sorry, I guess I don't know my own strength."

He rubbed his arm, feeling for skid marks. "I'll say."

"It must be the jujitsu," she explained.

"Gesundheit."

"No, jujitsu. It's a form of martial arts. I practice it with a videotape on the weekends. It's wonderful exercise." Paige fiddled with her eyeglasses and waited for him to hold still. She paused to smell her roses again. "It reduces stress."

"For you, maybe."

MAN OF THE YEAR

She grinned. "Anyway, about this fiancée scheme . . . well. I hate to do this to you, especially after all the candy and flowers—"

"And the pulling out of chairs and the compliments and the laughing at computer engineering jokes," he reminded her.

"Those, too," she agreed, "but I realized when we got to Guido's tonight that we'd made a big, big miscalculation."

Dread rolled in Brodie's middle like a bowling ball. "That's impossible," he bluffed, not really sure what she meant but unwilling to remain silent. "We're here, we're together, and my family loves you. What more do we need?"

"Compatibility. Affection," she began, ticking them off on her fingers one by one. "And that's just for starters."

Brodie, still stuck on the miscalculation idea, went on. "But you all hit it off. Shelby wants your cheesecake recipe before we leave here tonight. And my mother offered you that trial position at SupraTech, starting right away. And you took it, so . . ." A terrible thought struck him. "Paige, were you just using me to get into my family's company?"

He caught hold of her chin when she turned away from him. Brodie tilted her face upward, too horrified at the idea he'd just broached to notice the way her lips parted invitingly, as though in preparation for a kiss.

"I can't believe you would even accuse me of

that!" Looking disgusted, Paige wrenched her arm away. "How dare you?"

"How dare I? How dare I?" Hell, she was driving him insane, to the point of repeating himself. He had to end this, before it was too late. "I'll tell you how. Just like this: Did you use me to get a job at SupraTech?"

"You're serious." Paige gawked at him, too hurt by what he'd said to muster the more scathing response he deserved. "You really think . . . oh, this is useless! Brodie, you checked my credentials yourself. Do you really believe *I* used *you?*"

"No," Brodie admitted. "I don't. Sorry."

He ran his hand through his mussed-up dark hair and turned away briefly, staring toward the distant table where his family impatiently awaited their return. Even in profile, he looked gorgeous. Tall. Mysterious. Basically unattainable.

Oh, damn.

"It doesn't matter." Tightening her grasp on the tissue-wrapped rose stems, Paige did her best to sound decisive. "Your family isn't buying this, Brodie. Nobody else will, either. I guess I just don't have what it takes."

He looked genuinely surprised. "Don't have what it takes? To be a pretend fiancée?"

"To be *your* pretend fiancée," Paige clarified. "Nobody believes it. Did you see the way they were grilling me? And the way Shelby kept staring at my dress?"

"She was probably wondering if you were wearing something nicer underneath it."

Brodie scowled thoughtfully as he looked her up and down, and Paige had to force her hands to her sides to keep from covering up whatever he saw beneath her last-minute forty-percent-off evening wear.

"You have to admit," he added, "it's big enough for one and a half of you."

"It is not!" Self-consciously, she plucked at the slippery rayon fabric swishing around her thighs. Actually, it *was* a little bit on the baggy side, but it was just too bad if he didn't like it. "You're trying to distract me. It won't work."

"It's already worked." With unself-conscious grace, he leaned against the arch beside them and gave her a cheerful look. "Come on. Surrender, Paige. We've already been over this, and you're already committed."

"Or ought to be."

"Har, har." Brodie slipped his arm around hers and began guiding her toward the table where the Richardsons waited. "If you come quietly, I'll even share my tiramisu with you."

"No."

He raised his eyebrows. "You don't like dessert, either? No fancy shoes, no designer dresses, no pleading 'too full to eat a bite' while scarfing down chocolate from your date's plate?" Brodie paused. "Are you sure you're really a girl?"

"I'm sure I'm not the girl for you."

"Just because I don't like your dress?"

Just because you don't like me, Paige thought miserably. *All of me. And I'm really starting to wish you would.*

"No, just because we're not believable as a couple," she said aloud, digging her heels into the restaurant's tiled floor. "I'm not going back to that table. And you can't make me."

"Wanna bet?" Brodie waggled his eyebrows, looking devilish . . . and utterly irresistible. Just when Paige began to really wonder what kinds of incentives he might have in mind, he relented and returned to the shelter of their alcove by the phone. "Oh, all right. You're worried we're not believable as a couple?"

She nodded.

"Then what we need is a crash course in couplehood." Thoughtfully, he looked her over again, then nodded a decisively. "First, put your hands on my shoulders."

"Why?"

"Quit looking so suspicious. I'm not going to accost you between the pay phone and the take-out menus."

Hesitating, Paige bit her lip. With Brodie, a person never knew. As soon as she touched him, he might swoop in for another one of those amazing kisses, and she'd lose the will to resist altogether. Still, she'd promised to help him, and she'd already gotten a temporary SupraTech job out of the deal. Her conscience dictated a certain amount of reciprocation.

Ask for the deluxe treatment, she remembered April saying, *you deserve it.* So Paige did.

Quickly, before she could lose her nerve, she set aside her roses and brought up her hands to rest on Brodie's broad shoulders. His body heat seared through the ordinary navy fabric, imbuing it with an intriguingly masculine scent. His muscles bunched faintly beneath her palms, and when she dared to look up again, he was smiling at her.

"Very good," he said encouragingly. "Now kiss me."

"What? No!" She started to lift her hands away. "I should have known this was a trick, just some new way to coax a kiss out of me. You're a kissing maniac!"

"I'm not going to touch you. See?" Brodie gestured toward the two feet of empty air between them. "You're in charge of this, Paige. But you have to trust me."

Skeptically, she tilted her head, then sighed. After all, she had come this far. "Okay."

"Okay. Let's start smaller. Step closer."

Paige shuffled her feet, suddenly so sensitized to her surroundings that she felt every tiny piece of dust grinding beneath the soles of her pumps. Breath held, she looked up. "How's that?"

"Very good. Just a little closer. You need to feel comfortable being next to me."

As if *that* would ever happen! Nevertheless, Paige did as he suggested. Soon, she stood almost toe to toe with him. Their clothes brushed together, as though her dress and his pants and shirt were getting better acquainted, too.

"Great." Brodie's mouth hovered only a few

inches away, and his soft breath warmed her ear. "Can I put my arms around you?"

Silently, Paige nodded, too engrossed in the pounding of her heart and the yearning sensations she couldn't ignore to say anything more. She felt his arms cradle her waist, exactly as though she were a woman both precious and rare. *Wow.* Tentatively, she relaxed into his strong, steady grasp.

He rubbed his thumbs over her waist, then gave her a congratulatory squeeze. "See? That wasn't so tough, was it?"

"Well . . . unless you count the fact that my knees are weak, my heart is racing, and I can't seem to quit staring at your mouth," Paige answered without thinking. "Then, no. Not so tough at all."

Something that sounded very much like a groan escaped him. Paige couldn't tell for sure, because Brodie squashed her face against his chest for that one brief instant, and she was enveloped in a close encounter that rattled her even further.

"Do you always say exactly what you think, when you think it?" Brodie asked when he let her come up for air. "Because if this goes much further between us, I'm not sure I can take—"

"I don't know," she interrupted, testing the width of his shoulders with an exploratory squeeze as her courage returned. "I'm new at this."

"New?"

Oh, no. If he guessed the truth about her, all bets would be off. "New-ish," Paige hedged. "And anyway, I've never been the subject of this kind of . . . instruction before. What's next?"

"Move closer."

She did.

"Closer."

She did.

"A little more."

"Any more," Paige protested, "and we won't be able to draw a deep breath."

"I hope not."

"Oh. I see. " She complied, feeling slightly scandalous as she stepped between Brodie's spread feet and into the vee of his legs. Holding on to his shoulders for balance, Paige pressed her body all the way against his. *Double wow.*

Brodie raised his arm from her waist and peered at his watch. "I figure about five minutes of standing like this ought to catapult us straight into an instant comfort zone. You won't be shy about touching me anymore, and I—"

"You?"

"I won't have to worry about your getting cold feet and bolting out of our deal before the month is out."

"Sounds sensible," Paige managed to say. It was difficult, she discovered, to appear unaffected when pressed up against more than six feet of hard-bodied male. This was nothing like the typical end-of-date peck on the cheek she'd encountered now and then. "Clock's running, right?"

"Mmmm-hmmm."

His voice rumbled against her, drawing her attention to the curvy press of her breasts against his chest. *It's strictly for the sake of our deal,* Paige reminded herself. *It's instant physical bonding, and nothing more.* But that didn't make their contact feel any less wonderful.

Or any less right.

Her body heated, drawn to mold itself still further against every square inch of Brodie's chest and thighs and lean, khaki-covered hips. Dizzily, Paige registered the pleasant scratchiness of his emerging razor stubble where he'd rested his cheek against her temple, the steady thud-thud of his heart beating against her breasts, the subtle tensing of his leg muscles as he braced himself against the wall to support them both.

She inhaled the clean scent of his skin, savored the exciting pulse of her blood zipping through her veins, felt her nipples tighten and push against the sports bra she'd hurriedly pulled on before her mad dash from the Saguaro Vista press this morning, and wished that she'd thought to buy herself a fancy, lace-embellished bra along with the discount dress this afternoon.

As *if* Brodie would ever see it.

Compelled by the same mysterious allure that had drawn her earlier, Paige looked up into his face. His jaw was square and strong, topped by a fascinating mouth and a straight nose, and eyes that gazed into hers as though she and Brodie had waited a whole lifetime to be together like this. Enchanted by the idea, she raised her hand to his cheek. Felt herself rise up on tiptoes, stretching higher and higher . . . and then her eyelids fell closed as she neared the enticing warmth of Brodie's mouth, and began to anticipate the first brush of her lips against his.

A kiss was what she needed. Surely that would speed up this getting-to-know-you process nicely. With a quick silent prayer that she wasn't making a mistake, Paige stretched all the way up.

Moments before their lips met, Brodie jerked his head backward. He looked at his watch, gave her a puzzled smile, and then announced, "On second thought, I guess a minute and a half would be good, too."

Then he grabbed her roses, stuck them in her hand, and hauled them both back to the table for the rest of their command performance.

Six

By the time the after-dinner espressos, cheesecake slices, and squares of tiramisu had been delivered around their table, Brodie realized that Paige had been right. He really had miscalculated things, including the effect Paige herself would have upon him.

It's only lust, he tried to tell himself, remembering the press of her surprisingly curvy body against his. *The natural reaction of a man to a woman, when they are close enough to share the same breath.* The fact that he felt happy around Paige, that he felt an inexplicable urge to make sure she was happy, too, had nothing to do with it.

It sure as hell didn't mean he was falling for her. No way.

He could handle this.

"I'd say you picked another winner this time, Brodie," Ken Richardson announced from the end of the table. He winked at Paige, then leaned sideways and gave his son a hearty slap on the back. "Paige here is a great girl. I guess you haven't lost your touch, eh, Brodie?"

"Dad, don't get started."

"What?"

Brodie frowned, anticipating his father's unpardonable pride in him.

"You're a genius, son!" Unrepentant, Ken faced Paige again and explained, "Your fiancé here always did have a knack for picking a winner. Did he tell you about the first time he—"

"Dad!"

"—sent SupraTech to the top of the analysts' best-buy lists?"

Oh, God. Not the stock pick story again. Brodie winced and moved to short-circuit the anecdote before his dad could pick up speed. "It's ancient history," he told Paige. "Nothing you'd be interested in."

"Oh, but I am." Propping her elbow on the table, Paige pushed aside her uneaten dessert and rested her chin in her palm. "I want to know everything there is to know about my guy," she gushed. "Absolutely everything."

Geez. Leave it to Paige to play the adoring fiancée role to the hilt now, when he least wanted her to. "Really, I—"

"Come on, honey. Don't be modest," she said, pulling a comical face at him. "Let's hear what Mr. Richardson has to say."

"Call me Dad," Ken offered magnanimously. "You're practically part of the family."

Heads nodded in agreement all around the table. His mother even reached over to squeeze Paige's hand in encouragement, and his brother

Shane and Jules's stockbroker raised their wineglasses in a salute. Brodie groaned.

Paige beamed. "Okay . . . Dad. Please, tell your story."

"All right." Straightening self-importantly in his chair, Ken Richardson began. "It all started when Brodie was eight years old. Nora had just finished work on her latest prototype, a strap-on hand mixer that operated at the touch of a fingertip. Soufflés, mashed potatoes, that thing made 'em, easy as pie. She was all set to bring it to market, when Brodie here"—he gave his son a proud paternal punch on the arm—"toddled upstairs from the basement workshop—"

"Dad, I didn't toddle. I was already in grade school, for Pete's sake!"

"Who's telling this story?" his mother demanded. She smiled at Ken. "Go on, dear."

"He was carrying the remnants of an abandoned smart appliance project in his little fists."

"I was old enough to tie my shoes, walk to school, and lug home ten pounds of books in my backpack. I wasn't that little!"

Brodie's efforts to stop The Story in its tracks were useless. His dad only grinned and went on.

" 'Why don't you finish this one, Mom?' the kid asked. And so Nora took another look at it, finished up the design, and before long the Versa-Mix was launched."

"SupraTech's most profitable invention," Paige said. Awestruck, she gazed at Brodie. "And you picked it out?"

"Without our little boy, here, the Versa-Mix would never have happened," his mother confirmed. "We owe a lot to him."

"I was just a kid," Brodie argued. "It was a lucky guess."

"Followed by many more lucky guesses," his dad interrupted. "It got to be where Nora would line up the new inventions each season, Brodie would make his picks, and we'd launch them. Never failed."

"And now SupraTech is a multimillion-dollar company." Paige sat back, shaking her head. "I never even knew." She turned to Brodie with a thoughtful air. "I can't imagine why you never told me."

Here it comes. Next she would ask him to pick the winning lottery number. Choose the best job from a slew of offers. Select the one most likely to succeed from her assortment of yet-to-be-patented inventions. It was always the same. Once a person found out about his knack for picking a front runner, they started seeing him as a some kind of marketing genius, and things were never the same.

He wanted no part of it.

"I didn't tell you because I don't do it anymore." Leaning away from everyone, Brodie fiddled with his fork, discovered he no longer had an appetite for dessert, and stabbed the tines into the pillowy helping of tiramisu. "I've moved on to other things—"

"Like trips to the Caribbean, parties, skiing jaunts to Telluride, and parties," Shane put in.

"Not to mention regular treks to Europe, more parties, and a habit of never missing a good time." He grinned. "Did I mention the parties?"

"And the past isn't important," Brodie finished doggedly. He quickly used his napkin, threw it onto the table, and rose. "Except where it concerns the past couple of hours, which were terrific. Thanks for dinner, everyone. Paige and I have to be leaving."

At his urging, Paige got up, too, and after she'd gathered her bouquet of roses, they said their good-byes. On the way out, Brodie caught up with their waiter and dished out enough money to cover everyone's meals.

Paige watched him count the bills and press them into the waiter's palm. "Let me guess," she said. "Hush money, right?"

He blinked at her innocently. "I've got nothing to hide."

"Except your talent for business. Brodie, why are you spending all this time running away from success? Even if you don't want to work at SupraTech, I'm sure there are lots of companies that would hire you. In an instant. You could—"

"Become a corporate curiosity? No, thanks." He guided her outside, and they stepped onto the hot sidewalk into a sultry June night. The city lights of Saguaro Vista cast a glow into the desert sky overhead as they walked toward the parking lot, side by side. "There's more to life than spreadsheets and market forecasts and investments. More to life than work."

"You can't hide who you are."

Brodie glanced at her. "Nicely put, for somebody who's had a lot of practice doing that very thing."

"What?" Paige stopped, and her dowdy dress swirled around her. She scowled at him. "I do not hide who I am. I embrace it! Just because I didn't mention some of my credentials when I went for the position at SupraTech doesn't mean—"

"No, it doesn't," Brodie agreed. He stopped beside his roadster and dug out his keys. "That's not the kind of hiding I was talking about."

"What, then?"

Paige blinked at him from behind her glasses, looking genuinely puzzled, and equally appealing. What was happening to him? She wasn't his type at all, and yet . . .

"I was talking about this." Brodie grabbed a fistful of her skirt, and rubbed it between his fingers. "Hiding what I'm sure is a perfectly nice body—"

She snorted.

"—beneath enough fabric to pitch a tent with."

"Hey!"

"And this . . ." He released her dress and raised his hand to her hair, smoothing the silky strands away from her face. "Hiding your face behind all this hair. It's always in your eyes."

Paige swatted his hand away. "If you're finished criticizing me," she said quietly, "maybe we can leave. I have to get up early for my new job tomorrow."

"I'm not criticizing you. I'm just saying that with

a little effort, you could be an incredibly attractive woman."

She gaped at him. " 'Could be?' Is that supposed to make me feel better? Because if it is—"

"You're right." Brodie held up his hands. "I'm out of line. What's it to me if you like to go around pretending to be a plain Jane?"

"Pretending?"

He nodded.

"I'm not pretending! I have other things on my mind, that's all. More important things," she informed him, "than skin-tight dresses and dumb high heels and whether or not I should highlight my hair."

"Oh, yeah? What's on your mind, then?"

"Right now?"

"No, next week."

She made a face.

"Of course, right now."

"Well . . ." Paige fluttered her roses, staring down into their velvety red petals. She bit her lip, and shuffled from sensible shoe to sensible shoe. "Well. If you have to know, I've been thinking about finishing what *you* started, back in the alcove at Guido's."

That sounded promising. Intrigued, Brodie paused in the act of opening his convertible sportscar's door. "You have? Why don't you go ahead and do it, then?"

"Because! I'm not the assertive type, that's why," she replied, not meeting his eyes. "I can't do it."

A sense of disappointment welled inside him.

Telling himself it didn't really matter, and not believing a word of it, Brodie opened the driver's side door. Then he turned back to face Paige, ready to escort her to the passenger's side.

"I just don't have it in me," she said, "to do *this*."

With a wobbly lunge, she wrapped her arms around his neck, shoved them both back against the hood of the car, and in the deepening twilight of an extraordinary Saguaro Vista night . . . Paige somehow found the courage to kiss him senseless.

Brodie's tactics must be rubbing off on her, Paige decided the following morning. How else to explain the way she'd, well, *manhandled* him last night?

What she'd told him was true, Paige reflected, spinning her office chair away from the computer she'd been working on. She'd never been much good at asserting herself.

This very morning, in fact, when she'd arrived at SupraTech for her new temporary position, had she protested the cramped and isolated cubicle she'd been assigned? No. Nor had she argued when another of the product designers had dumped a low-level upgrade project on her, or when the engineer in the cubicle next to her had arrived and begun blasting hip-hop music from his computer's speakers. So what in the world had come over her last night?

It had to be Brodie's influence. Or maybe all

those kisses he'd given her. They'd jumbled her neural pathways.

At this rate, she'd be useless for anything but contemplating the width of her for-the-moment fiancée's shoulders. The dazzling effect of his smile. The endearing way he did his best to fulfill every one of her fantasies about being sought after.

With a sigh, Paige reached into her pocket and pulled out one of the rose petals she'd impulsively stashed there this morning. She rubbed its soft, delicate surface with her fingertip, remembering the pleased look on Brodie's face when he'd given her the bouquet. If only his thoughtfulness had been real . . . .

Someone popped their head over the top of her cubicle wall. "Cruller?"

Paige blinked at the maple-frosted goodie being waved back and forth in front of her eyes. Hurriedly, she slipped the telltale rose petal back into the pocket of her suit, and then glanced up to see the SupraTech receptionist, Jennifer—of the long, perfectly coiffed blond hair and expertly manicured fingernails—hovering outside her cubicle.

"Even temp workers have to take a break sometime," Jennifer went on, nodding toward the cruller. "Want one?"

"Actually, the high proportion of simple carbohydrates in that wouldn't be the best thing for me right now," Paige said regretfully. She tapped the computer monitor in front of her, upon which the 3-D upgrade model spun, waiting for her next input string. "And then I wouldn't get this upgrade done for the Blenda-whirl II. Thanks, anyway."

"Is that a no?"

"I'm afraid so."

"Oh, well. Maybe next time." With a shrug, Jennifer came all the way into Paige's work space, then grabbed a stack of engineering data sheets from the cubicle's sole chair. "Got a minute?" she asked, holding the documents in the air as though preparing to sit down.

"Sure." Paige took the data sheets and stacked them beside the phone, then waved for the receptionist to get comfortable.

A little company actually would be nice. She'd begun to feel invisible, stuck back at her faraway desk. Ordinarily, feeling invisible suited Paige just fine. But today, for some reason, it only made her feel . . . lonely. Something was definitely happening to her.

But what?

"Aren't you abandoning your post, though?" she asked, determined to distract herself from her thoughts. "What if somebody comes in?"

Jennifer waved away her concerns, munching the maple cruller. "There are two of us," she replied when she'd finished the first bite. "Tag team receptionists."

Paige grinned. "Good. Then we have time to talk."

And talk they did. By the time the cruller was gone, and Paige finished her second cup of green tea, she and Jennifer were fast friends. They'd cov-

MAN OF THE YEAR 91

ered SupraTech's remarkable twenty-five year history, the ups and downs of most of the people in the company, the likelihood of finding a date-worthy man on the job, and the short version of Paige's college years. Jennifer had just launched into a fascinating description of the upcoming SupraTech twenty-fifth anniversary events when something, some disturbance in the far-off front of the building, reached them both.

Murmurs rose and drifted back to them, along with the occasional giggle—and once, a high-pitched, girlish squeal. Next came the sound of multiple desk chairs creaking as their occupants turned to view the cause of the hubbub, followed by a sudden, inexplicable wash of fragrance. It was as if a thousand department store perfume ladies had descended upon SupraTech, and were spritzing their way toward Paige's cubicle.

Jennifer sniffed. So did Paige. "What the heck?"

Her new friend only smiled knowingly. "Must be Brodie."

"Huh?" So far as Paige remembered, Brodie smelled nothing like a field of flowers—and he definitely didn't smell like an upscale perfumery. "What do you mean?"

"You'll see," Jennifer said mysteriously.

Very soon, she did.

Brodie's voice reached her before he did. "Paige?" he called, sounding forlorn. "Paige, are you back here?"

More conversations buzzed. The perfume smell

grew stronger. In preparation for the next olfactory assault, Paige sucked in a deep breath of less flowery air. "What should I do?" she asked Jennifer.

"Answer him!"

But she couldn't. Shy Paige Mulvaney, yelling across entire rows of cubicles? That kind of attention she could do without. Especially on her first day on the job.

She settled for awkwardly bobbing upward, hoping to see Brodie. In fact, she did see him—along with an entourage of female SupraTech employees who'd followed him here into corporate Siberia. They swarmed in his wake, at least a dozen strong, armed with lipsticks they were busily applying or perfume they were earnestly dabbing on, fluffing their hair, and scribbling down numbers on scraps of paper.

One intrepid woman whom Paige recognized as a member of the product testing department wrote something on a sticky note and stuck it on Brodie's sleeve. *Her phone number,* Paige realized as he peeled it off and smiled at the woman. He was as irresistible as maple icing on a cruller.

"Amazing," she whispered.

And he wanted *her.* At least temporarily. The sheer improbability of it was enough to make a girl feel downright irresistible herself.

He rounded the corner leading to her cubicle. When Brodie spotted her peering above the low wall, a broad grin spread over his face. Wasting no time, he strode through the rest of his entourage and stopped in her entranceway.

"Come on," he said, holding out his hand in invitation. "Let's get out of here."

Seven

"You really didn't have to do this," Paige said as they walked hand in hand from the SupraTech building. "I'm capable of providing my own lunch, you know."

"I know." Swinging the paper sack he'd brought in his free hand, Brodie gazed down at her, taking in her prim suit and no-nonsense demeanor. Today she'd swept up her hair into some kind of twist at the back of her head, probably intending to look more businesslike. Instead, Paige somehow looked softer. More approachable.

More like the woman who had surprised him with a mind-blowing kiss last night. He liked that woman a lot.

"But," he continued as they reached the sidewalk and went on, "we have to make our engagement story look real, don't we?"

"Oh, that's right. Our 'engagement.'" For a moment, she looked sad. Then Paige squeezed her hand in his and blinked up at him through her horn rims. "Well, that's fine, then. Your taking me to lunch will make it look doubly real."

"So will this."

Stopping in the shade of a sidewalk tree, Brodie pulled her into his arms, then eased his palm along the back of her neck and tilted her face upward. Not caring who was watching, or even if anyone was, he lowered his head and indulged the curiosity that had kept him running around in circles all morning.

Yup, he realized as Paige moaned softly and returned his kiss with the same passion he remembered—last night had not been a fluke. He wanted Paige Mulvaney.

And he would stop at nothing to get her.

"Kiss me again," he murmured. "Ahhh, Paige. You feel so good."

Brodie lowered his hand, skimming over the curves and softness concealed beneath her loose-fitting suit. He reached the hem of her jacket, and made fast work of the few buttons that kept it fastened all the way to the collar of the shirt she had on underneath. With a wild sense of anticipation, he slipped his hand inside, to her waist. He flexed his fingers and, moving his mouth to the side of her neck for a few slow, nibbling kisses, steadily moved his hand upward.

The weight of her breast filled his palm. Instantly, her nipple hardened. Groaning, Brodie cupped her more fully, feeling the slide of her silky shirt against his skin . . . feeling his sense of self-control retreat with each moment that swept past.

"Mmmm . . . you taste good, too," he said, kissing his way from her neck to her earlobe. Gently, he bit down on the sensitive flesh there, and Paige shivered in his arms. Her response felt real. True and innocent and infinitely more provocative than any other he'd experienced.

Had he ever really found her plain at all?

Right now, it was hard to believe.

"Oh, Brodie! Shouldn't we—I mean—" Her head moved, arching slightly to the side. "I don't even think anyone is watching. Shouldn't we save this for a later time when someone's around to—"

"I don't care who's watching." *Or if anyone is watching at all.* At the moment, his phony engagement plan was the last thing on his mind.

Right behind finding out if kissing the other side of Paige's neck would make her moan in exactly the same way, and discovering whether or not she felt even an iota of the attraction he suddenly felt for her.

"But—oh . . . ."

Her protests dissolved beneath a new, heart-stirring kiss. Kissing Paige, Brodie had discovered, was new each time. Even more exciting. And a total surprise. Unlikely as it was, he couldn't seem to get enough.

On the street beside them cars whizzed past, their drivers intent on noontime meetings or finding a place to eat before their lunch hour ran out. The breeze stirred up dried mesquite bean pods on the sidewalk, and sent them skittering past their feet toward the SupraTech building. A moving van rumbled by, followed by a huge truck.

The blare of its horn jerked them apart.

Brodie released Paige just in time to glimpse the

truck's bearded driver giving them a salute as he zoomed down the street followed by a blast of diesel exhaust.

"What are we *doing*?" Paige asked. Looking appalled, she straightened her jacket and glanced backward toward SupraTech. "If anyone sees us—"

"They'll believe we're a happily engaged couple." Smiling, he smoothed her still-crooked jacket lapels. "What's the problem with that?"

"What's the problem?" Paige started walking, purse swinging as she strode purposefully down the sidewalk. "The problem is that I don't generally stand around on street corners making out with men I barely know!"

Brodie tried to look repentant. He felt pretty sure he failed. "Fine. What else do you want to know about me?"

"Arrgh!"

"Okay, okay." Breaking into a jog, he caught up with her. Doing that, unfortunately, ruined the very nice view of her feminine, side-to-side walk. He caught Paige's hand. "I'm sorry. I couldn't help myself."

She cast suspicious eyes on him.

"Really," he insisted.

"Sure. And I can't keep turning down these job offers I've been getting from the NBA." Exasperated, Paige swiveled as she walked, keeping her barely five-foot, four-inch body constantly in motion. "Come on, Brodie! Am I really supposed to buy a line like that?"

"It's not a line."

"It must be!"

"Why?" Brodie asked. He crushed the handles of the brown paper shopping bag he'd been carrying more tightly in his fist, driven to distraction by her aggravating refusal to believe him. "I can't keep my hands off you, Paige. It's as simple as that. As soon as I get within touching distance of you, something happens to me. It's as if my body has a will of its own."

She paused at the edge of a wrought-iron gate set into a creamy stuccoed wall. With one hand atop the latch, Paige gave him a serious look. "And what does your brain have to say about all this?"

"Not very much," Brodie confessed. "The old mental processes pretty much shut down whenever I'm around you."

"Are you saying that you're attracted to me against your will?" Shaking her head, Paige wrenched open the gate and they both walked down a meandering paved path, through a courtyard landscaped with desert plants. "Gee, that's really terrific."

"It could be terrific," he said, ignoring her obvious sarcasm. "If you would just give it a chance."

"And then what?" She stopped beside a wood and wrought-iron bench placed in the shade and plopped her purse onto its seat. Facing him with her hands on her hips, Paige went on. "We'll *really* fall in love, and we'll really get engaged, and we'll live happily ever after?" She shook her head, looking regretful—and painfully serious. "We're both smarter than that."

"Paige, come on. We could—"

"Or at least one of us is."

Well, he couldn't really blame her for digging at what she supposed was his weakness. Still, her remark hurt. For the first time, Brodie began to regret the playboy reputation he'd worked so hard to establish. "That's not fair."

"Sure it is." She busied herself with rummaging around in her purse. "Before this goes any further, we might as well face facts. We don't have anything in common. Our chances for a lasting relationship are—" Suddenly, Paige threw up her hands and sat down on the bench, hauling her purse onto her lap. "Listen to me. A lasting relationship. Ha! I don't even know why we're talking about this."

"Because there's something between us," Brodie answered. "Unlikely or not. It's undeniable."

"I don't feel a thing," she denied instantly.

"You're lying."

"I am not!"

"You are." He took a seat beside her and set down his shopping bag on the ground between their feet. "Do you want to know how I know?"

Paige pressed her lips together and shook her head.

"I know you feel something for me," Brodie went on, "because your smile gets all big and goofy—"

"Hey! I resent that."

"Whenever you see me. Just like mine does, whenever I see you."

"That's ridiculous." Head down, Paige pulled

out a paperback book and a crumpled brown paper sack from her purse. "There's no evidence to suggest—"

"Look."

"What?"

"Look at the evidence."

Slowly, she raised her head. For once, her hair couldn't shield her face, and Brodie silently thanked the hairstyling gods. Studying the half-suspicious, half-hopeful expression Paige wore, he felt another wave of hopeless infatuation. Just as he'd expected, a silly, lovestruck grin burst onto his lips.

It was matched by one very much the same, from Paige.

She gasped and ducked her head again.

"And I know you feel something for me," he continued relentlessly, "because you relax when we're together. You quit marching around like a corporate soldier on parade, and just . . . lean into me, in a way that makes me feel . . ." Brodie paused. He was unable to believe he was about to utter something this sappy, out loud, in a public place. ". . . like a hero."

"Well, there's no denying you're a nice guy. After all, you did brave your throngs of admirers at Supra-Tech to take me to lunch." Putting on an elaborately carefree expression, Paige opened her wrinkled paper sack, withdrew a sandwich, and offered him half. "I hope you like turkey on wheat, because that's what's on the menu today."

Brodie didn't care about the menu. There really

was something going on here, between them, and he needed to get to the bottom of it.

"There are other signs, too," he persisted. "You listen to me when I have something to say. When you think I can't see you, you give me a sexy little *hmmm* kind of look. And it makes me hope that I bring out the sensual side in you that no one else knows about."

Her cheeks reddened. "Brodie, come on—"

"And," he finished triumphantly, "you always tilt your head in exactly the right direction when we kiss. So there!"

"The fact that we don't bump noses signifies true love? Look, I'm not the most experienced at this dating stuff, but—"

"But nothing. This might have started out as some kind of phony arrangement between us, but now it's real."

"About as real as Kenny Brewster's invitation to my senior prom, I'll bet." Shaking her head, Paige sighed and offered him the sandwich half again. This time, Brodie took it. "I'm not falling for that one twice."

"Who's Kenny Brewster?"

She waved away the question. "Nobody important. Let's eat."

"Really. Who's Kenny Brewster?" If he was going to entertain fantasies of breaking the creep's dancing legs for hurting Paige's feelings, however long ago, Brodie wanted to know who he was. "Tell me."

Chewing a huge mouthful of turkey sandwich,

Paige pantomimed, being unable to speak. She shrugged her shoulders, as though to say, sorry—too busy eating to indulge your macho protective instincts. Brodie waited for her to finish, and was stymied again when she took another big bite.

He grinned at her bulging cheeks. "Okay, I can take a hint. We'll talk later."

Looking relieved, Paige opened her paperback book—something by a currently popular relationships expert—and began to peruse it. With practiced motions, she ate and read, balancing the book effortlessly on her lap while she juggled her sandwich and shared the prepackaged munchy vegetables Brodie had brought from a nearby deli. Every bite or so, she turned a page, frowning in concentration.

"Do you always do that?" he asked.

She put her thumb on the page to hold her place and looked up. "Do what?"

"Read."

"Of course not. The pages get wet if I read in the shower."

Brodie grinned. "I mean, read while you eat. You haven't quit turning pages since you started devouring that sandwich."

"Oh." Momentarily, she looked puzzled. She glanced from the book on her lap to the vegetables, container of pasta salad, and unopened bottle of white wine arranged on the bench between them, and wound up on the sandwich in his hand. "Yes, I guess I do. You mean you don't read while you eat?"

"No."

"Hmmm." Paige leaned over and peered into Brodie's nearly empty shopping bag. She seemed surprised to find that there wasn't a novel—or maybe a glossy brochure on the benefits of vacationing in Aruba—stashed inside. She wrinkled her nose, a motion which made her glasses slide down. Pushing them up, she said, "What's wrong with reading?"

"Well, when you have company for lunch, it's considered polite to occasionally speak to them," he teased. "Unless the etiquette expert my mother hired to tutor me in seventh grade was just making that up, which is a possibility. She also told me that nice girls expect nothing more than a handshake at the end of a first date, which I've found to be . . . well, let's just say, inaccurate."

Brodie grinned, and gave her legs an exaggerated leer.

Paige tugged the hem of her beige skirt over her knees. "I'll just bet you have. Your real dates probably don't stand a chance against you."

"Are you saying I'm irresistible?" Filled with a new sense of hope, Brodie playfully plucked the book from her lap and dog-eared the page to mark her place. He snapped it shut. "That's a theory I'd love to explore with you. Later." He winked. "But first, I want to know about this reading habit of yours . . . and about Kenny Brewster."

She looked trapped. Apparently choosing the lesser of two evils, Paige primly folded her hands in her lap and explained. "Everyone in my family reads constantly. When I was growing up, my father usually had papers to grade for his students." She made an unsuccessful grab for her book. "He's a physics professor at the University of Arizona. And my mother has always reserved dinnertimes to read professional journals. She's a statistician."

"Let me get this straight. When you were a kid, you all used to sit down to dinner, pick up your books or journals or papers, and spend the whole meal in silence?"

"Well, of course it was silent. Otherwise we would have been too distracted to read." Giving him a *sheesh!* look, Paige dipped a baby carrot into the ranch dip and munched into it. She shrugged. "At least we didn't argue at the dinner table like some other families."

"Sure. That's a plus." Nodding, Brodie tried to go along with her view. But he just couldn't. The family meals Paige described sounded too chilly, too intellectual, emotionally empty. No wonder she felt awkward at times. She'd had no practice being sociable.

And you've had too much practice at it, a little voice jibed. With a frown, Brodie ignored it. He'd created his party-hearty persona for a perfectly good reason, and he wasn't ready to let go of it yet.

No matter how shallow it seemed since he'd met Paige.

"Why do you think I come here?" she asked, waving a celery stalk to indicate the two-story stucco building to their right, around which the benches, pathway, and landscaped plants rose. "I feel at home here. This is the quietest place I know."

Brodie squinted at the letters carved onto the building's side, just below an inset clock. "The Saguaro Vista City Library?"

"You must be familiar with it." Paige's arched brow suggested otherwise, as though any man who spent his days on tropical islands wearing baggy surfer shorts and sunglasses couldn't possibly understand a library. "Aren't you?"

"Sure." He retrieved the corkscrew from the sack at his feet and started to open the wine. "I think my parents donated a new wing a few years ago."

She actually believed him. Brodie peered out from behind the hank of hair that had fallen into his eyes when he'd bent in concentration over the wine bottle, watching as Paige's eyes grew rounder behind the lenses of her horn rims. With a little sound of dismay, she lowered the dip-covered snow pea she'd been about to crunch into.

"You *think*?" she asked. "Haven't you even been inside the library to see it?"

He shrugged. "You know us jet-setters. Never enough time between parties for the so-called important things." Taking care to seem ultra happy-go-lucky, Brodie filled two paper cups with wine and gave one to Paige. "Don't you read the tabloids?"

"No. And even if I did, I wouldn't believe everything I read. I never do." Thoughtfully, she sipped her wine. "For instance, the *Territorial* reported that you were honored last year for making a donation to the International Children's Coalition, when I know perfectly well that particular organization doesn't accept monetary donations."

"It wasn't money that I donated."

"It wasn't?"

The fact that she looked so astonished galled him. It was time, Brodie decided, to turn the focus away from himself. At this rate, Paige would pry out all his secrets, his hedonist façade would crumble, and people would start expecting him to turn up at SupraTech on a regular basis again.

Worse, they'd start expecting him to make decisions.

"Checking up on me, hmmm?" he asked. "I'm flattered."

She looked a little flustered. "No, I just happened to be looking at some chip technology information in the computer archives at the library for work this morning, and I was searching the back issues of the *Arizona Territorial* anyway, so—"

"So you snooped on me." Brodie grinned. "Awww. I didn't know you cared. You're making me feel all mushy now."

She blushed in the face of his teasing. "I don't see anything wrong with bolstering our fake engagement story with a little information." Distractedly, Paige drained her paper cup and held it out for a refill. "That's all I was doing."

"Mmmm-hmmm." He held her hand to steady it as he poured more wine into her cup, lingering over the brush of his fingers against her skin . . .

and the warm, soft feel of her body leaning toward his. Then Brodie reluctantly released her, pulled a white waxed sack from inside his shopping bag, and held it aloft. "Ready for dessert?"

"What's that?"

"Truffles." He opened the sack, and the rich scent of chocolate wafted upward. "The candy shop downtown makes the best pecan caramel truffles I've ever tasted. Have one."

Paige paused over her selection, and then lifted one eyebrow upward. "You think of everything, don't you?"

Brodie nodded, encouraging her to choose a truffle. It wasn't until she'd selected one and bit into it that he went on. "You know, some people claim that chocolate is an aphrodisiac."

She swallowed her first bite, coughing as it went down. "What does that have to do with anything?"

Smiling, Brodie looked into her eyes. "Simple," he said. "I wanted to know if you agree."

Eight

Brodie could be tenacious, she'd give him that, Paige decided after they'd finished lunch and had returned to the SupraTech building. She'd managed to evade his questions about the aphrodisiacal properties of chocolate truffles and had steered the conversation toward one of the twenty-fifth anniversary celebrations instead.

For a while, it had worked. Brodie had actually devoted some time to describing the event he was scheduled to appear at later that day—a ribbon-cutting ceremony for the new personal robotics section—and to answering Paige's questions about his role at SupraTech. But now . . . well, he seemed to have something else on his mind.

Beside her, Brodie swiped his entry card through the electronic lock on one of the building's offices. With a subtle click, it snapped open. He planted his hand beside the plaque reading Vice President on the door, and ushered them both inside.

"Wow, nice digs." While Brodie raised the window blinds, Paige took in his luxurious office, with its plush carpet, polished desk and credenza, and cushy chairs. There was even a leather sofa along one wall, with framed artwork above it. Experimentally, she sat on one corner of the sofa and gave a little bounce. "Even your seating is comfortable. Very posh."

"I know. My parents spared no expense in trying to lure me here to work." Brodie lifted a cut-crystal jar from the edge of the desk and raised its lid, indicating the brightly colored candies inside. "Including regular restocking of M&Ms, my favorite. Want some?"

More chocolate. Yikes. "I'd better not. Thanks, anyway."

She was in enough trouble as it was, wondering whether or not the feelings she'd been having for Brodie were real, whether or not he really found her as sexy as he seemed to . . . and whether or not the leather sofa had room for two.

Actually, she mused, if she put her purse on the floor and scooted backward, and if Brodie stretched out and held her in his arms, they just might . . . .

Aaack! What was she thinking?

Panicked at the overwhelming appeal of her fantasy, Paige rose. "I really ought to get back to work. You vice-presidential types might be able to get away with long lunches and wearing beach clothes to work—"

He cast a perplexed glance downward at the We Be Jammin' T-shirt he'd picked up in Jamaica, and his loose-fitting athletic shorts and sneakers.

"But we lowly engineers can't," she finished, and hurried toward the door.

MAN OF THE YEAR 111

Brodie stopped her halfway there. He wrapped his arm around her chest and dragged her toward him, like a stage manager hauling a vaudeville act away from the footlights with a giant hook. She shivered at the contact, and felt herself being turned to face him.

"I've got 3-D modeling to finish, and a whole stack of updates waiting to be reviewed," she protested halfheartedly. "All that work will—"

"Will wait." He smiled down at her, looking . . . well, looking kind of goofy and happy, just as he'd suggested at the library courtyard. He also looked as though he'd guessed she'd been trying to escape him—and he wasn't about to let her off that easily. "I've got a few more things to go over with you," Brodie said. "So you might as well get comfortable."

In a wink, she was divested of her suit jacket and purse. The items sailed toward the sofa and landed in the corner—right beside the sense of invulnerability she'd felt sure she'd possessed when she'd come into his office.

It must have been an illusion, Paige realized as Brodie wound his finger around a tendril that had escaped from her French twist. Because there was no way she could be invulnerable and still feel every pulse of her heart, every gasp of her quickening breath, every quivering, excited atom in her body launching into full-tilt celebration when Brodie touched her. She was only human. Only a woman, with a woman's heart and a woman's wish to feel treasured and wanted and beloved.

Of course Brodie didn't love her, she reminded herself sternly, standing steady beneath the continual, wildly flattering appraisal he gave her. But now . . . just now it seemed as though he wanted her. And a part of Paige was all too eager to grab this moment and wring all the memories from it that she could.

"That's better, isn't it?" he asked, nodding toward her abandoned suit jacket and purse as casually as though he undressed women in his office every day.

She took a deep breath.

"Ummm, it's fine." *Coward!* Rocked by the feeling of his stroking hand, now moving from her hair to caress her shoulder beneath her short-sleeved rayon shell, Paige tottered beside him. "Mind if I take off my shoes, too?"

Brodie raised his eyebrows. "Not at all. Make yourself comfortable."

"Because I feel a little wobbly," she explained as she slipped out of her navy pumps and bent over to align them, toe to toe, beside a filing cabinet. "It's probably just the wine we had." *And not your sex appeal making me woozy.* "I'm not used to drinking at lunch, or—whoa!"

His hands cupped her derrière, startling her in mid-sentence. "Sorry," Brodie murmured, sliding his broad palms slowly up to her waist. "Couldn't help myself. Did you know," he added conversationally, "that you have a really adorable backside? Nice and round and—"

"You d-don't say." Rapidly, Paige straightened,

giving up fussing with her shoes. Her shaky reply had not, she feared, conveyed the same nonchalance as Brodie's. Gamely, she went on anyway. "I can't say I've given my backside much, ahhh, thought."

"It's cute. Almost as cute as the way you start babbling when you're flustered."

"I do not babble. Or get flustered. Ever. Babbling is undisciplined and, ummm, getting flustered is ridiculous, so I really don't think I would—"

"Of course you wouldn't." His grin called her bluff. "And I apologize if I offended you."

"Thank you."

"And just to show that there are no hard feelings, I'll even throw in a concession." Brodie's cheerful expression warned her that whatever he was about to propose, he thought it would entail the one thing he seemed to live for. Fun.

"What's that?"

"You can cop a feel right back," he offered, grinning. With a Chippendale-worthy swagger, Brodie turned his back to her and looked over his shoulder. "Go ahead. Use both hands, if you want. Turnabout is fair play."

Amazingly, Paige managed to raise her eyebrow, just as though her brain wasn't ninety percent occupied with ogling him. "It doesn't quite feel like revenge when you're anticipating it this much."

"You're right." Reluctantly, he straightened. "Why don't you catch me by surprise sometime, instead?"

As if. "Thanks, but I—" She suddenly remembered she was trying to play it cool and folded her arms over her chest instead and kept quiet.

"Hey," Brodie went on, giving her ear an affectionate tweak, "you never know. One of these days, I just might unleash your inner wild woman."

Feeling out of her depth at the very idea, Paige headed for the temporarily Brodie-free security of the sofa. "I don't think I have one." She sank onto the cushy, embracing leather and gazed up at him. "An inner wild woman, I mean. I've been so busy with studying and school and work—those three degrees didn't just materialize for me, you know—that I haven't had time to develop her."

Wistfully, she clasped her hands in her lap, then stared down at them. Those hands had never held a lover against her, keeping him close in the night. They'd never teased a man, or stroked him with the intimacy that she'd imagined but never known. They'd never gripped fistfuls of sheets as ecstasy shook her, or caressed the man she loved with the freedom born of experience and tenderness.

For that, all at once, Paige felt indescribably sad. She'd missed so much, and had never really realized it until now.

The sofa cushion tilted as Brodie plopped beside her. Paige didn't look up as he captured her hand in his and twined them both together. He arranged their hands atop his hard-muscled thigh and gave her a squeeze.

"Sensuality isn't something you have to develop," he said quietly. "It's there, inside you. Waiting to be enjoyed. Waiting to be discovered."

Abruptly, she realized exactly how much she'd almost revealed about herself. At this rate, he'd guess the truth, and she'd become nothing more than a curiosity to him. Again. Paige didn't think she could bear that.

Waving her free hand, she attempted a world-weary sigh. "Oh, I've discovered my, uhhh . . . you know. Sure I have. It's not that. I just mean that I haven't discovered it *lately.*"

"Mmmm-hmmm." Speculatively, he squinted at their joined hands. A few moments passed, then Brodie transferred his suddenly serious gaze to her face. "Well, wild and crazy Paige, I'd be honored to refresh your memory. If you think you might let me."

She couldn't breathe. Had he guessed? Did he know? If this was an offer motivated by pity, Paige figured she'd rather gnaw her way through the walls of the SupraTech building than accept it. But if he meant it as sincerely and tenderly as he seemed to mean it . . .

"I don't know, Brodie," she murmured, afraid to look at him and uncomfortable with the feelings he aroused in her. "Maybe we shouldn't make this any more complicated than it already is. Maybe we'd be better off—"

"Just letting it slip away?" He shook his head, and tightened his grasp on her hand. His thumb stroked soothingly over the back of her wrist, and the delicious warmth of his body was enough to melt what little self-control she still possessed. "I can't. I won't. I don't know why I feel this way about you, Paige. It doesn't make sense—"

"Gee, thanks a lot."

He kissed away the frown from her lips and then went on. "And it sure as hell doesn't fit into my plans."

"You have plans? I'm impressed."

"But I have to know what this is between us."

"Curiosity," Paige said firmly, relieved to diagnosed his behavior at last. "That's all it is. Plain, ordinary curiosity."

Brodie frowned. "There's nothing plain or ordinary about the way I feel about you."

"Novelty, then," Paige guessed. "You've never been involved with a woman whose IQ was higher than her bra size, and then I came along."

"Yeah. You and your three college degrees." He released her hand and stood, then paced toward the desk. The crystal jar clattered as he dug out a handful of M&Ms and popped a few in his mouth. Keeping his back to her, Brodie said, "Let's just lay off the intellectual superiority routine, okay?"

"Okay. I'm sorry." Stricken that she'd said something so thoughtless, Paige pushed herself off the couch and followed him. Tentatively, she laid her hand on his shoulder, feeling his rigid muscles tighten still further at her touch. "But I didn't mean it the way it sounded, you know," she said. "I think you have a lot to offer. You're funny and sexy—"

He turned at that, and his renewed scrutiny

made her blush. To hide it, Paige raised her other hand, too, and kept her head down as though fascinated by the sight of her fingers sweeping over the broad muscles hidden beneath his T-shirt.

"And charming," she finished, "and you'll probably make some girl very happy someday."

"Just not you. Is that what you're saying?"

"Well . . ." *Why is he asking me something like that?* Frowning, she absentmindedly traced her fingertips up his chest, across his shoulders, and down the warm length of his bare arms, then back again. Up, across, down . . . she almost whisked her hands to the untucked hem of his T-shirt, eager despite their situation to glimpse again Brodie's washboard abs. At the last minute, Paige stopped herself and answered his question instead. "I'm not saying that at all. I was just pointing out your good qualities."

"Yeah. You sure were." With a meaningfully arched brow, Brodie captured her wandering hands and pulled them away from his body.

With shock, she realized that her explorations had actually rumpled his clothes—he looked as thoroughly manhandled as he had last night atop the hood of his Mercedes convertible. What had gotten into her?

"Unfortunately," he went on, releasing her hands, "you seem to think my good qualities are pretty limited. Or that I'm good for only one thing. Well, you've gotten closer than most. For what it's worth."

She was stunned into silence. Why lumping her

with ninety-nine percent of the rest of the single female population of Saguaro Vista and beyond should have felt like an insult, Paige didn't know. She only knew that it did.

It did, and it hurt.

The only thing worse was leaving Brodie behind, rumpled and surly and inexplicably disappointed, and knowing that, somehow, she was the cause of it all.

Nearly a week later, Brodie's mood had predictably lightened but Paige's determination to find out where she'd gone wrong hadn't eased in the least. Sure, he'd been insulted by her low opinion of him, but it hadn't been until she'd done the fingertip cha-cha over his chest and mentally undressed him that he'd really gotten steamed.

Could it be that he expected to ogle her, kiss her, tease her, and tempt her . . . and not be ogled, kissed, teased, and tempted in return?

Nah, Paige decided as she put the finishing touches on her five o'clock, post-workday hairstyle in the SupraTech employee ladies' room and shoved her comb back in her purse. Brodie was a red-blooded man. The *most* red-blooded of them all, according to April, who kept up with the news. There was no way he didn't expect—and appreciate—a little sexy reciprocation. So what was the problem?

"Jennifer," she asked, catching her new friend's eye in the mirror they were sharing, "what do you know about Brodie?"

The receptionist laughed. She paused in mid-tease, holding her can of hairspray aloft over her blond tresses. "What *don't* I know about Brodie? That would be a better question. I've known him for a long time."

"Well, what I mean is . . ." Unsure how to phrase her question, Paige stopped. She sucked her lower lip between her teeth and thought about it. "Is Brodie sensitive about his reputation?" she finally asked. "About being a playboy and all that?"

"Sensitive? Why should he be?" Jennifer closed her eyes and spritzed on a cloud of unscented super-hold. "He's rich, he's famous—"

Paige winced, remembering the onslaught of reporters and photographers she and Brodie had faced last night, just trying to leave the twilight performance of the Saguaro Vista symphony together. Fame, she'd learned during her first week with him, wasn't all it was cracked up to be.

"And he's still willing to leave it all behind by marrying you, right?" Jennifer recapped her hairspray and applied a swipe of deep pink lip gloss. "Near as I can tell, Brodie has no reason to regret his past, wild as it was."

Wild? That sounded intriguing. And like something she ought to know about. With the same tantalizing feeling of discovery she experienced every time she came up with a new twist to a programming theory, Paige pounced on Jennifer's comment. "Well, how wild was he? Really wild? I mean—"

"Wild enough to break into the ladies' room to hurry along his fiancée," came Brodie's teasing voice. It boomed from the tiled walls, and made both Paige and Jennifer jump.

She turned in surprise to see him striding into their pink and white powder room, looking twice as masculine here where he wasn't supposed to be. Fortunately, everyone else had long since left.

That was Brodie for you, Paige decided—breaking the rules at every turn. Even his clothes were different than expected—a crisp white buttondown shirt, low-slung blue jeans, and casual shoes—a combination that surprised her with its uncharacteristic neatness.

She still wanted to know what wild things Jennifer had been about to reveal about him, of course. But at the moment, all Paige could think about was how he looked right now. The most coherent way she could describe the overall effect he made was . . . *yum.*

"You look gorgeous," he said, apparently reading her mind—and doubling the sentiment, if his lingering look was any indication. For a pretend fiancé, his admiration was very convincing, even to Paige . . . who should have known better. She was finding her grip on humdrum reality harder and harder to maintain.

"But we don't have time to stand around swapping rumors," he said. His censorious look made it plain that he'd overheard their conversation, and didn't appreciate it much, either. "We're meeting the Saguaro Vista Home Show representatives for cocktails in half an hour—and they can't wait to meet my new fiancée."

Paige sighed at his reminder of their shared obligation. Impressing the home improvement industry was a necessary part of ensuring SupraTech a place—and twenty-five more years—in the market for future smart appliances. But that didn't mean she had to like it—or like sharing Brodie, in the process. Their time together was too short, too precious to be frittered away with daydreaming about things that could never be.

Sheesh. Would she never learn?

"I'm almost ready," she told him, turning her attention to the mirror for one last hair check as Brodie watched.

The gesture was a mistake. Their combined reflections only reminded Paige of the contrast between Brodie's effortless urban sophistication and her own lack of style. Making a face at her image, she turned toward Brodie again.

With a wiggle of the fingers of his outstretched hand, he beckoned her closer. He grinned. "Let's go, before Jennifer comes up with more dish on me."

"Ha, ha," said the blonde, slanting him a lighthearted look. "Your secrets are safe with me, Brodie, and you know it."

That was what Paige was afraid of. Feeling disappointed and strangely guilty for snooping on him, she snatched up her purse and let Brodie usher her through the ladies' room door.

Next time, she promised herself. Next time she'd find out *exactly* how wild Brodie had been.

And maybe, once she knew, she'd even be inspired to try a little wildness herself—before their time together ended, and it was too late to indulge.

Nine

With one hand on the small of Paige's back, and a good portion of his attention on the appealing view she presented in her pale blue suit dress, Brodie frowned over his shoulder at Jennifer as they left the ladies' room.

He pantomimed zipping his lips in a silent appeal for quiet, but the receptionist only shrugged.

"This was all your idea, remember?" she whispered.

He did. Only too well. He remembered enlisting Jennifer's help when he'd wanted to acquire a devil-may-care new image. He remembered, too, that at the time, securing the cooperation of SupraTech's biggest gossip had seemed like a good idea.

Maybe he really was as brainless as Paige seemed to think.

"Just lay off for a while," he muttered to Jennifer, letting Paige go ahead. "Before you and your stories talk me right out of a fiancée."

"I thought it was a set-up," she said, speaking low enough that only Brodie could hear. The three of them passed through the SupraTech lobby and into the heat of a summertime desert evening. They headed for the parking lot.

"I was there when you came up with this scheme, remember?" Jennifer went on. Then she paused, looking at him with something that came aggravatingly close to amazement. "Don't tell me you're serious now? Unreal. Bad boy Brodie has actually gotten himself hooked! Ha!"

"Shhh!" He thrust a hand through his hair and cast a worried glance toward Paige, walking a few paces ahead of them now. Near as he could tell, she hadn't overheard their conversation. "I've just had enough of the wild and crazy reputation I cooked up. That's all."

Jennifer shook her head. "Uh-uh. That's not all. I've known you a long time, Brodie. Long enough to know when you're smitten with someone—"

" 'Smitten?' Come on—"

"And long enough to know when three's a crowd." She dug out her car keys from her purse, and headed toward the far edge of the parking lot. "See you later, Paige. Brodie. Have a good time tonight. I'm off to happy hour!"

He needed to take matters into his own hands, Brodie decided, once he and Paige had left their meeting with the home show representatives. It wouldn't be enough to get Jennifer to stop talking up his swinging bachelor image—especially since Paige's opinion had already been formed. Somehow, he needed to make her change her mind. He needed to make Paige see the other sides to him.

Unfortunately, at the moment, she seemed most interested in just one of those sides—the outside.

Sealed beside him in his convertible, Paige rested her head back and watched him drive. He felt her gaze glide over his hands, his face, his shoulders . . . his thighs. Perhaps thanks to the double cocktails she'd had earlier tonight, she was glowing with confidence and good cheer. Suddenly she seemed easier and a lot more comfortable with him.

Probably, Brodie thought sourly as he gripped the steering wheel more tightly, that was because Paige thought she understood him now. He was only some kind of a . . . a boy toy to her!

In aggravation, he drummed his fingers on the steering wheel. Didn't she think he had a mind, a heart, a soul? Was it too much to ask that Paige notice, and maybe even appreciate, those parts of him, too?

Hell, he was just a man. A man who wanted something more than ogling and come-ons and wanton nights. Just a man, who needed, suddenly, to be taken seriously by the one woman in the world he hadn't been able to charm into doing things his way.

Just a man, who'd actually broken into a sweat because of the heated glances demure Paige Mulvaney was sending his way. What was happening to him?

She leaned closer, washed in brightness and

shadow from the glow of the streetlights and storefronts they passed. Her scent teased him, subtle and feminine and real . . . and all the more dangerous for it.

"You look really terrific tonight, Brodie," she said. "You clean up"—her gaze dipped from his partly unbuttoned shirt collar to his denim-clad legs—"very nicely."

The low purr of her voice aroused him, setting his imagination spinning. She would sound just like that, Brodie thought, speaking from the pillow next to his. Her fragrance would waft from the sheets on his big empty bed at home exactly the way it did from the soft leather seats of his convertible. Her hand would caress his knee just the way it was doing right now, and . . . .

And it wouldn't be enough.

This time, with Paige, he wanted more.

"Thank you," he rasped, keeping his vision focused on the road. Gently, Brodie raised her hand from his knee and lifted it, then pressed his lips to the fingers she'd curled trustingly around his. "I just threw on whatever came to mind first," he lied. "You know us guys—the grab and sniff method always works for us."

"Mmmm-hmmm. Whatever you say." Her smile said she didn't believe a word of it, almost as though Paige knew about the hour and a half he'd managed to spend getting ready for her tonight.

Who'd have thought that his usual routine could be extended so easily into a showering, shaving, trying on clothes, mouthwash-swilling, burning

MAN OF THE YEAR 127

himself with the stupid iron extravaganza? Not him, that's for sure. Frowning down at the faint scorch mark that still decorated the sleeve of his shirt, Brodie realized that maybe, possibly, things had gotten out of control.

He'd never ironed for a woman in his life.

At this rate, he told himself as he steered around the corner and neared their destination, he would find himself dragged to antique stores on the weekends, missing football and basketball games for the privilege of holding his 'fiancée's' purse while she paid too much for dusty knickknacks and rickety old furniture. At the thought, Brodie shuddered.

Or at least, he tried to. Truth was, doing just about anything by Paige's side sounded pretty good to him.

"Oh, God," he muttered. Jennifer had been right. "I've got it bad."

"What's the matter? Are you lost?" Putting the finishing touches on words sure to raise the hackles of every man over the age of sixteen, Paige pushed her horn rims higher on her nose and fumbled in the glove compartment for a Saguaro Vista street map. "I think I saw a club back there, a few blocks away. The Purple Posh. If you turn around here, maybe we can—"

"We're not going to a club."

She blinked. "More cocktails? I swear, Brodie, I'm not sure I can—"

"We're not going for cocktails, either."

"Well, I think maybe we should avoid private parties for the time being, too," she said. "Especially after what happened with the reporters who followed us to your friend Malcolm's birthday bash the other night."

Brodie grinned. "Their cameras only got a little bit wet in the swimming pool," he said. He pulled the car to a stop and turned off the ignition. "Besides, we're not going to another party tonight."

"We're not?" She blinked again, looking temporarily discombobulated by the idea that they might not be doing anything involving a crowd, loud music, and revelry—and her looking sexier than any woman covered from below her knees to her collarbones had a right to. "Why not?"

A terrible thought struck him. "Are you sorry we're not?"

"No!" Paige said hastily. She smoothed the wrinkles from the map and put it back into the glove compartment. "As long as we're together—I mean, as long as we're keeping up the engagement ruse, what difference does it make what we do?"

"None at all." Now that he wasn't distracted by driving, Brodie couldn't help but fix all his attention on her. She'd left her dark hair loose, he'd noticed, and it flipped up in a sassy way on the ends—a styling suggestion from Jennifer, wielder of the mighty hairspray, he'd guess. He opened his mouth to tell her how much he liked her new look.

Instead he said, "I feel like I've been waiting all day to touch you."

Her gaze softened, looking suspiciously misty. "Oh, Brodie. That's so . . . well, the truth is, I feel the same way."

And it was true. He did want to touch her. Never mind that he hadn't exactly meant to blurt it out that way. Or that he'd risked hearing her burst into laughter at the mushy sentiment behind the words. Never mind any of it . . . because in the next moment, Paige leaned over the gearshift to press her lips to his, and Brodie felt as though he'd never had a mind at all.

Thoughts fled beneath the tentative brush of her lips against his, pushed away beneath the heat of their mouths coming together and their breath mingling and their hearts racing in sync. Groaning, Brodie kissed her with all the newly discovered need in his soul, and knew that if this was his one chance to hold on to the woman he needed, he would do whatever it took to keep her.

Including what came next.

They broke apart, finally, and Brodie worked for a minute to unscramble his thoughts. Then, as soon as he could form a complete sentence again, he said, "Museum. Close soon. Got to go in."

"What?"

Okay, so maybe complete sentences were too ambitious, Brodie realized. He settled for pointing through the steamed-up windshield at the sign on the building directly in front of them.

Paige read it. "We're going to the art museum?"

He was in luck. She looked delighted. Giving himself a mental high five for discovering a common interest, Brodie nodded. "Yes," he said. "We definitely are."

* * *

After much maneuvering, Paige finally managed to catch up with Brodie sometime later in an alcove beside a cluster of Remington bronzes. He looked a little panicked at her approach, probably at the determined look on her face, but rallied quickly.

Just as he had for the last forty-five minutes or so, he smiled that sappy, happy smile of his—the one that made her heart pound in her chest—and then he took her hand and turned them both to contemplate the nearest sculpture.

Staring blindly at the bronze cowboy on horseback, Paige wanted to scream with frustration. Sure, she liked art as well as the next person. But tonight?

Tonight, she had other plans.

Her friend April had given her a new piece of advice—an addendum to her original 'seize the day' dating manifesto—and tonight, bolstered by a new outfit, restyled hair, and two Pink Lady cocktails, Paige intended to take it.

Go for it.

In that spirit, she cozied up next to Brodie, making sure their joined hands accidentally brushed her thigh. "It's nice and quiet in here, isn't it?" she ventured.

"Mmmm-hmmm."

"And private."

"Mmmm-hmmm."

"In fact, I haven't seen anybody since we came in."

"Me, neither." He angled his head sideways, staring harder at the Remington sculpture. The serious expression on his face made his profile even more angular and intriguing than usual. Brodie . . . the thoughtful yet hunky man of the month. Briefly, he slipped his gaze to her. "Nice piece, isn't it?"

Paige stifled a grin. "Yes." Running her finger over the sculptured cowboy's permanently whirling lasso, she asked, "You do realize that tonight's date won't be followed by a quiz, right?"

"Ha, ha." He made a face at her, but some of the tension left his shoulders, and for that she was glad.

After that, Brodie toured the art museum with a little more ease . . . and a lot more evasiveness. Every time Paige tried to brush up against him, slip her arm around him, or even—by the time closing time was near—hold his hand, he dodged her. At this rate, her attempts to 'go for it' were getting her nowhere.

What was the matter with him? All of a sudden, he seemed more interested in discussing the Cubist movement and American sculptured realism than in getting closer to her. If she hadn't known better, Paige might have believed that what he wanted most from her was a meeting of minds.

She took another look at him as they entered the museum's last room, a showcase of paintings by local artists. No, Paige decided. This was a man made for other kinds of meetings altogether.

This was a man who could, quite possibly, help her over the hurdle of her embarrassingly long-lasting . . . situation. It was something she'd been thinking about for a while now. And why not? Brodie was friendly. Charming. Sexy.

And you love him, a part of her chimed in. *Which is the best part of all.*

Rattled by the notion, Paige smoothed her hands over her dress and made one last attempt to follow April's advice. She drew in a breath for courage, and joined Brodie beside a landscape painting of a rain-soaked desert spiked by lightning. And said, "Nice painting, but I'dratherbesomeplacealonewithyou. Whatdoyousaywegetoutofhere?"

Whew! She'd gotten it said, exactly as she'd practiced all those zillions of times between breakfast two days ago and cocktails tonight. Filled with relief, Paige gazed giddily up at Brodie, awaiting his response.

"Huh?" he asked. "I didn't catch most of that."

Embarrassment steamrollered right over her sense of relief. But, now that she was already committed, Paige figured she could do nothing but repeat, "I'd rather be someplace alone with you. What do you say we get out of here?"

That goofy grin of his disappeared—only to reappear an instant later, with an even more dazzling intensity. She began to believe this assertiveness stuff might really work.

"Sure," Brodie replied. "I'd love that."

* * *

Saguaro Vista's Coffee Cup Café was eclectically decorated with retro furnishings, a black, white, and red-accented color scheme, subtle lighting, and upholstered booths in hound's-tooth check. At eleven o'clock at night, it was nearly deserted.

It was also the last place in the world Paige expected to find herself.

Especially when she'd just been called upon to answer the last question in the world she wanted to address right now.

"Maybe I didn't hear you right," she told Brodie, holding her fingers steady in the midst of dunking a teabag into her black cup. "You want to know *what?*"

"I still want to know," he repeated, leaning further over the tabletop they shared, "who Kenny Brewster was."

"That's what I thought you said."

"Well?"

"Well, what?" she hedged, busying herself with a packet of sugar. Nervously, Paige flipped it back and forth, watching the little packet's swinging arc in the dim light from their table's pendant fixture. "There's nothing to tell, really," she finally said, unable to bear the silence any longer. "Kenny Brewster was just a boy I knew once. End of story."

She ripped open the sugar packet and dumped its contents into her tea. She grabbed her spoon and stirred, watching the hot liquid spin and swirl—and trying to appear as though she had nothing to hide.

Which was, of course, ridiculous.

And Brodie knew it.

"Back in the library courtyard," he said, "when we had lunch that day, you said our relationship was, I quote, about as real as Kenny Brewster's invitation to your senior prom. What did you mean?"

Paige sighed. Obviously, delaying the inevitable was impossible. "I meant that I don't want to be a sucker twice. You want to know who Kenny Brewster was? He was the boy I had my first crush on. The president of the debate club, the cutest member of the chess team . . . the boy who, after four years of hoping, finally invited me to the senior prom."

Brodie made a sympathetic face. "Did you have a bad time? High school is usually torture, I know, but—"

"No, I didn't have a bad time." She waved away his sympathy. Someone like him would never really understand the hoping, the longing, she'd experienced. "I didn't have any kind of time at all. It seems that Kenny Brewster only invited me as a joke, on a bet from one of his buddies, who didn't believe anyone could actually want to date the class brain."

"Oh, Paige . . ."

"Which probably explains," she concluded fiercely, "why I spent prom night all dressed up, with my new hairstyle and borrowed jewelry and pinchy high-heeled shoes, sitting beside the window at my parents' house, waiting for someone who never showed."

Brodie plucked the spoon from her hand, forcing her to stop stirring. Tenderly, he closed his fingers around hers. "He was a moron. I could still break his legs. Tell me where he lives."

A wan smile touched her lips. "No, thanks."

"Because I will," he went on, deepening his attempts at a tough guy voice. "It's the least the creep deserves for hurting you."

With great effort, Paige managed a shrug. "It was a long time ago. And even with that little dating snafu in college—"

"What dating snafu in college?"

"The one where the frat boy pretended to invite me to an all-night keg party . . . and I waited to meet him at the wrong address for two hours before I figured out what was going on." Miserably, Paige slurped some tea. "I figure that doesn't mean I'm doomed, or anything. Date-wise, I mean."

Brodie grimaced. "You fell for it twice?"

"Hey!" She straightened in her seat, and cast him a defiant look. "Statistically speaking, the odds of such an event happening twice were extremely low."

"I'm sure."

She sighed. "It shouldn't bother me, I guess." Gazing outside the café window at the moonlit shops and offices lining the street, Paige thought about her past. "After all, it's over with now. And since then I've had several perfectly successful dates. A steady relationship later in college, even, with a non-frat boy. So I'm fine."

"Are you?" Brodie looked concerned. Why did

he have to turn all sensitive and extra-caring now, when she really could have used the ego bolstering effects of a passionate kiss? Or at least a nice ogle? "I mean, you seem fine, but—"

"I am." She drew a deep breath, and was surprised to find herself feeling shaky. "It's just . . ."

"Hmmm?" he encouraged. "You can tell me."

"Well. It's just . . ." Damn. Could those really be tears prickling behind her eyes? Now? Blinking rapidly, Paige stared down at her tea and tried to get herself under control. "It's silly, but I've always regretted that night. After all," she said wistfully, "you only get one shot at your senior prom."

Silence settled around them, and in that long moment, Brodie reached toward her. He cupped her face in his hand, and the warm feel of his palm against her skin was as soothing as anything she'd ever known. Slowly, he thumbed away a silly, telltale tear from her cheek, and his next words were slow and sure.

"That's true, Paige. And if I could, I'd make it up to you." Through her tears, she glimpsed his sincere hazel eyes and wonderful smile. "But since I can't . . . would it help if I told you I'm falling in love with you?"

Ten

"I must not have heard you right," April said, looking up from the bowl of egg whites she was beating for her latest gourmet creation, a tequila-lime tart. Their apartment was fragrant with the tangy zing of freshly-squeezed citrus, and, of course, tequila. "He said *what?*"

"That he was falling in love with me," Paige repeated. She tried to squelch the delighted grin that rose to her face at the remembrance of Brodie's surprise revelation, and failed. What she really wanted to do was break into a happy dance, all around the kitchen. "Can you believe it?"

Her roommate dropped her whisk into the bowl. "Sure, I can. You're lovable." She smiled. "What I can't believe is that you waited almost three weeks to drop this bombshell on me, your best friend! When did you plan to break the news? When you phoned me from your honeymoon hotel?"

"Hold on," Paige said, feeling her natural sense of caution kick in. "Let's not get ahead of ourselves here."

Even now, after having lived with Brodie's amazing news for the duration of three weeks at Supra-

Tech, four 'fiancée' press appearances, several Richardson family get-togethers, various dates with the man himself, and one twenty-fifth corporate anniversary 5K run at which she and Brodie had both finished in the middle third and celebrated with ice-water toasts, she could hardly bring herself to believe it. Brodie was actually falling for her!

"There's not even a wedding planned," she went on, reining in her excitement once again. "Much less a honeymoon."

"It's a matter of time." April resumed whisking. "Just so you know, we redheads don't look our best in coral, orange, or mustard yellow."

"April—"

"In fact, if I could choose the color, that would work better for me."

"Whoa! Bridesmaid's dresses?"

"Sure." Blithely, April spooned the snowy beaten egg whites into her bowl of tart filling and began to fold them in. "First comes phony engagement, then comes true love, then comes bridal registries, bachelorette parties, and bridesmaid's dresses." She paused. "You know, if I weren't so happy being single, I might be jealous of you."

Extroverted, man-magnet April, jealous of *her*? Paige's mind boggled at the very idea.

"I don't see you spending too many nights all by yourself," she pointed out. "You're great at this dating stuff! Which is why, by the way, I need your help with this."

She leaped up from her seat at the kitchen table, too jumpy to sit still any longer, and grabbed the item she'd indicated. At her touch, the plastic covering crinkled, nearly obscuring the logo of the expensive department store on the packaging.

April raised her eyebrows. "You need help with your dress? Your new, knock 'em dead, month's worth of salary, designer dream?"

Paige cast the fanciful, palest pink gown a despairing glance. "My dress, my hair, my makeup—" She clutched her lank hair and moaned. "Everything!"

"Okay, don't panic. We'll have you looking gorgeous in no time."

"No time?"

"Well, a little time." April grinned as she spooned pale green filling into the waiting tart shell. "After all, we want you to look extra ravishing tonight. If I know you—and I'm pretty sure I do, after all these years and all those pints of ice cream we've devoured together—that look in your eye means something. I'm betting it's either that you're going to finally abandon that vestal virgin routine of yours—"

"April!"

"Or you're going to tell Brodie you love him back."

Paige gasped.

"Or possibly both."

Regaining a little of her usual calmness, now that she'd enlisted April's help in preparing for tonight, Paige grinned back at her friend. "Possibly."

With the glamour demons temporarily at bay, she felt ready for almost anything.

Ready, even, to take the chance of a lifetime.

Believing that a sought-after, drop-dead gorgeous, charismatic guy like Brodie Richardson could really, actually, finally be in love.

With her.

"I think I'm going to pass out." Brodie moaned the words into his cell phone, feeling himself break into a sweat beneath his black evening clothes. "I should have brought a paper bag to breathe into, like Mom always said."

"That's for hyperventilating," his sister-in-law Shelby remarked on the other end of the phone line. "If you really feel like you might pass out, put your head between your legs."

Feeling desperate, Brodie did. His forehead connected with the steering wheel of his convertible, nearly making his prediction a reality. "I can't," he muttered into the phone. "I'm in my car. But now I have a really spiffy lump on my forehead, which ought to bring Paige to her knees over my devastating good looks."

"I've always said," Shelby offered, "that a little humility would do you wonders."

He groaned. "Are you sure Bryan isn't there? I'd really rather talk to my brother about—"

"No, he's golfing with Jules and her stockbroker. They're coming to the SupraTech bash later on. Fashionably late, as they always say."

Terrific. Brodie made himself unclench the steering wheel, then worked on loosening his rigid grip on the phone. This was what he got, he guessed, for actually seeking brotherly advice for the first time in his life.

Tonight's party—the pièce de résistance of Supra-Tech's twenty-fifth anniversary celebration, and the most public of them all—was important. Really important. Because tonight was the night he hoped would give Paige the memories she'd longed for.

An image of her as she'd looked during their conversation at the Coffee Cup Café rose in his mind, as wistful and heart-wrenchingly sad in memory as it had been in real life. *I've always regretted that night,* she'd said. *After all, you only get one shot at your senior prom.*

"Look," Shelby said, breaking into his thoughts. "Cut the dramatics and just drive on over there. Pick up Paige and—"

"I'm already there." Brodie looked through the windshield at Paige's apartment building. In the fading sunlight, the shadows lengthened, giving a sense of mystery to the evening. "I've been parked here for half an hour."

Shelby made a sound of disgust. "Then go in!"

He held the phone away from his ear, then eased it back into position when her outburst faded. "I can't."

Brodie had the sure sense that somehow, tonight, his life was going to change forever. A premonition, a prediction . . . he didn't know what to call it, and he didn't care. He only wanted to know he was doing the right thing.

"You're waiting to make sure you're doing the right thing, aren't you?" Shelby accused.

He jerked and stared at the phone.

When he didn't reply, Shelby went on talking. "Well, there isn't any one right thing, so you might as well go and get her. Have fun tonight, Brodie. And try not to worry. She'll say yes."

Suspiciously, he frowned toward the apartment complex again. "Say yes to what?"

"You mean you're not going to propose to her?"

He pulled at his suddenly tight shirt collar, fidgeting with his necktie. "We're, uh, already engaged, remember?"

Shelby, of the inch-long red manicured fingernails, high maintenance hair, and shopaholic's wardrobe, simply sniffed. "Come on, Brodie! None of us bought that phony fiancée story. We just liked Paige, that's all."

Great. His cover was blown, too. "Mom believes it."

"Only because she wants to make you happy. Now, enough procrastinating. Go get Paige. And make her happy tonight."

"I intend to try." Brodie waggled his eyebrows and tried to sound lusty, as though all he cared about was snuggling up to Paige and giving her his very best. Unfortunately, the nervous cracking of his voice didn't sustain his rapidly disintegrating carefree bachelor image. "Really," he said more quietly. "I'll do my damnedest to make her happy."

The last thing he heard before gathering together all the things he'd brought and stepping out of the car was Shelby's voice before she hung up. "Good luck," she said.

Brodie just hoped he wouldn't need it.

It took twenty-three minutes—time Brodie spent twisting an unwanted bottle of beer between his palms and gazing anxiously down the hallway of Paige and April's apartment—before Paige finally appeared.

To him, it was worth every minute.

He rose as she stepped into the dim hallway and came into view. With a nervous, half-bashful smile on her face, Paige paused at the entrance to the living room, unsure whether to come forward.

"Wow. You look . . . beautiful," he said, too awestruck by the sight before him to manage anything more.

"Thank you." Not meeting his eyes, she made a jittery grab for the chiffon wrap April held out to her. "We'd better get going," she blurted, coming closer.

"Wait." Paige looked up in question, finally meeting his eyes.

"First I want to look at you," Brodie said. "Longer."

And, at her shy nod, he did. Lovingly, he drew in the wonder of her, of her amazing eyes and her newly glamorous hair and the column of pale pink silk that followed her curves from her shoulders to her strappy high heels. Suddenly, he wanted to ease away the two thin straps that held the gown to her shoulders. Wanted to watch the fabric slide over her smooth bare skin and puddle at her feet. Wanted to lose himself in her warmth, in her body, in her.

But more than all that, he wanted to do what he'd come here to do.

Brodie bent, and from the table beside the sofa, retrieved the things he'd brought with him. First was his old high school class ring, which he'd retrieved from the forgotten depths of his sports locker. Next was his old varsity letter jacket, also from the days of his high school football stardom. He lifted the ring and slid it onto Paige's finger.

The weight of it dragged her hand downward, and she laughed, cradling it amongst the chiffon of her wrap in the palm of her other hand. "Does this mean we're going steady?" she asked.

"Something like that." Smiling, his heart filled with happiness, Brodie draped the letter jacket over her shoulders, and then pulled out the final item he'd brought.

"A corsage?" Looking suspiciously misty, Paige gazed at the plastic-encased orchid he was struggling to open. "You brought me a corsage?"

"Well . . ." He wrestled with the plastic, and finally succeeded in freeing the spray of tropical flowers. "You see, I wasn't there in time to break Kenny Brewster's legs. And I wasn't there to drive up to your parents' house and steal you away from beside that window. I couldn't bring you to the prom all those years ago, Paige," he said, "but—"

"Oh, Brodie! I-I—" She sniffed, blinking rapidly.

"Stop! You're going to make me ruin my new makeup."

"But," he went on, raising the corsage to pin it, ever so carefully, to her dress, "I can bring the prom to you now. Say you'll go with me. I'll be the envy of everyone there."

"Yes! Yes!" April suddenly screamed, beside herself with excitement. Grinning from ear to ear, she grabbed her roommate's arm and shook it. "Paige, say yes!"

"Oh, Brodie." Paige raised her hand and touched her new corsage's fragile petals with trembling fingers. For one terrifying moment, Brodie thought he'd done the wrong thing. That somehow, without knowing it, he'd done the one thing that could wrench her from him forever. But then she smiled up into his face, and the joy in her expression was a reward greater than any he'd ever known. "Yes, I will."

On their way out, her next whispered words went straight to his heart—and told him that he had, indeed, done the right thing. "Thank you, Brodie," Paige said. "No one's ever . . . well, let's just say, I'll remember this night forever."

All he could do was tighten his arm around her waist and guide them both into the star-spangled depths of that night, and hope she was right. "So will I."

Brodie framed her face in his hands and paused between kisses to give her a smile that managed to shine right through the shadows in the hotel parking lot outside the SupraTech gala. "Do you want me to stop, Paige? I'd rather not this time, but . . ."

His words dissolved into a groan as she lowered her head and kissed him. She wanted feelings, not words. Sensation, not thought. And tonight, she meant to have it all. Brodie apparently agreed, because he tangled his fingers in her hair and kissed her right back, in a way that left her dizzy and needing.

Never had she felt like this. Never. And, remarkable as it seemed, Brodie felt just as out of control as she did. He wanted her . . . and had for some time, if his words could be believed.

So that's what his behavior had been about these past few weeks, Paige realized dimly, trailing her lips from his mouth to the edge of his jaw. Brodie had been trying to get to know her better—and all the while, he'd been fighting an urge to—well, to do what they'd been doing ever since sneaking out of the party and to the relative privacy of his car.

"I don't want you to stop," she murmured, emboldened by the knowledge that he really, truly desired her. "I want to feel your hands here"—she demonstrated by taking his hand in hers and pressing it against her breast—"and here." Boldly, she slid his other hand to her hip. "Everywhere."

"Gladly." Deepening their kiss, Brodie spread his palm over her breast. He thumbed her aching nipple into a pinpoint of yearning, making the taut peak press against her dress. With his other hand, he hiked up her long skirt—already gathered around her bent knees and over his lap, spilling onto the car seat—and caressed her bare thigh. "Ahhh, Paige. I love the way you feel."

"I love the way you make me feel. Ohhh . . ."

He went on kissing her, went on touching her, and the heated rasp of his palm against her skin made Paige writhe atop him. He raised both hands to her breasts, stroking and loving and watching her response through dark, passion-filled eyes, and she arched helplessly forward to meet him. This was what she wanted. What she needed. To be touched as though she were precious and incredible and absolutely irresistible.

Fragments of orchestra music reached them, muffled by the steamy car windows. Flashes of light danced over them, as newly arrived partygoers drove past and then parked in some distant corner of the crowded lot. The scents of perfume and flowers and Brodie's tangy aftershave surrounded them in still more sensation . . . and none of it mattered, beside the overwhelming need she felt to be as one with him.

His hands were magical. His fingers, his mouth, his strong arms holding her against him, all combined in an exhilarating, intoxicating blend of male and female, desire and need. His thighs strained beneath her, strong, hard, and sure. Moaning, kissing him again, Paige caressed Brodie's wide, powerful chest and tugged at his shirtfront.

His necktie had long since been hurled into the tiny space behind the convertible's two seats. His cummerbund had followed, and now she was determined to see still more clothes shed. Brodie was absolutely wearing too much tonight. She needed to feel his skin against hers, now.

"Ahhh, Paige. Wait. Wait." He gasped, as though they'd reached their disheveled, passion-rumpled state by jogging across the parking lot, rather than by making out like two people who couldn't wait another minute to touch. "We should . . . we should go someplace really private. This isn't—" He touched her cheek, then raised the hand she'd persisted in using to unbutton his shirt and kissed it. "I want this night to be perfect for you."

"Then don't stop touching me."

He tilted her chin up, distracting her from the task of trying to peel away his half-unbuttoned dress shirt while Brodie was still wearing his suit coat. In frustration, Paige looked into his face . . . and the passion she saw there made her fingers clench in the starched cotton beneath her hands. She went still.

"I won't stop," he promised. "I'll touch you all night. Over and over again, until we're both too exhausted to move, and too satisfied to do anything but lie around and grin. Okay?"

With a promise like that, Paige figured, a girl didn't need to know much else. Especially when it came from the man she'd been falling in love with for weeks.

With a newfound assertiveness that astounded her, she plucked up the car keys from the console between the seats and shoved them into Brodie's hand. She smiled and kissed him.

"I thought you'd never ask," Paige said. "Let's go."

Eleven

By the time they rounded the corner leading to Brodie's hideaway house outside Saguaro Vista, the sky had clouded over and raindrops drummed against the cloth roof of the convertible with an intensity that matched Paige's heartbeat. Set against the night sky, the silvery drops glimmered down the still steamy car windows, sparkling as though lit from within.

That was how she felt, Paige realized. Lit from within, illuminated by love and the warmth of Brodie's caring for her. His hand rested possessively on her thigh, smoothing the silk of her dress and igniting a shocking need to feel his fingers stroke higher, caress longer, make her feel even more wild than she already did.

"Hurry up," she said, reaching for him herself. If she tried, she decided, she could probably have his suit coat and dress shirt off, have him halfway naked before he managed to shut off the engine.

"Soon," he told her, and the word was a rumbled promise that she'd have everything he'd mentioned before . . . and more.

Paige could hardly wait. Brodie shared her impatience, because he wrenched the car to a stop in the wet driveway and got out, leaving the keys jingling in the ignition. She watched him cross in front and come around to her side, and then he was there, opening her door, scooping her into his arms, carrying her with long, powerful strides through the rain and into the house.

It was like being the princess in every fairy tale she'd ever read, like being Eve and Aphrodite and the hottest, sultriest movie star, all rolled into one. With sexy whispers and more promises of all they'd share, Brodie carried her through the living room, past shadowy furniture and jumbled furnishings and down the hallway. She sensed the need in his stride, tasted it in the urgency of his kiss and the tight grasp of his hands. In the bedroom, he leaned toward the bed and carefully lowered her . . . and then quickly followed her down.

Cottony cool linens met her back. Hard, hot male met her front, strong and needful and wonderfully aroused. A comforter of colors she couldn't discern hugged them both in its soft embrace. Pillows flew as they embraced and rolled, reaching to shed damp clothes and kissing between explorations of bare skin uncovered, between moans of pleasure and surprise, between murmured words of need and desire and possession.

Suddenly, Paige stopped him. Rising into an almost seated position, she groped toward her dress front. "My corsage. It's special. I don't want to crush it."

At her words, he warmed the room with lamplight—bright enough to see that her orchid remained, fragile and perfect—low enough to seal her and Brodie together in the moment. With shaky fingers, he unpinned her flowers and set them safely aside, then raised her hand and kissed it. Brodie rubbed his thumb over the old-fashioned class ring he'd given her, and smiled.

"Are you sure about this?" he asked. "Because I've waited so long, Paige. I don't want to stop."

Brushing a kiss over his lips, lowering her hand to his knee, Paige answered truthfully, "I've never been more sure of anything. Please, Brodie. Make love with me."

It was as though her request redoubled his need—and hers, too. They embraced again, this time with even more heat, more passion, more urgency. Silk slithered as Brodie's skillful fingers made short work of her gown and high heels. All were tossed beside the bed, followed closely by one pair of men's dress shoes—joining his wrinkled, rain-drenched tuxedo jacket and pants on the floor—and the white flight of Brodie's dress shirt sailing toward the shadows beyond the mattress.

Sighing with pleasure, Paige ran her hands over his chest and shoulders, feeling the muscles there bunch and flex as Brodie held her. She felt his wet hair sweep across her shoulder. His mouth claimed her breast, and his hands held her to him as he went on loving her, now kissing and stroking, now dipping his hands lower to caress between her thighs until she was shuddering and yearning, wild with the need to love, and be loved.

She was still moaning, still reaching for him, when Brodie murmured something about protecting her. He reached for a condom and sheathed himself quickly, then returned to her, even more aroused than before.

"I love you," Brodie whispered, stunning her with the intensity and wonder of his declaration. "I love you, I love you, I love you."

And then he came back into her willing, eager arms . . . and proceeded to show her exactly how much.

Sunlight streaked over the furnishings in Brodie's bedroom, highlighting his rustic pine furniture, the occasional painting or potted cactus, his wonderfully mussed, delightfully occupied bed . . . and the woman he couldn't seem to get enough of, giggling beneath the sheets.

"Stop, stop!" Paige shrieked, emerging from between the layers of white linen with her hair askew, her glasses crooked, and her naked body tantalizingly half-revealed. He'd never seen her look more gorgeous. "I can't take any more!"

"That's not what you said last night," Brodie growled, lunging forward to trap her between his spread thighs. He tickled her until she gasped beneath him, then he sat back on his haunches and regarded her fondly. Maybe it was time to give Paige a break—so long as it wasn't a break long enough to allow her to launch her own tickle at-

MAN OF THE YEAR 155

tack, as she'd done shortly after they woke up. "Last night you couldn't get enough of me."

She smiled back at him, and borrowed time by straightening her glasses. That accomplished, Paige gave him an arch look. "Yes, well," she said blithely, "that was last night. And besides, I've always been a speedy learner. Speaking of which . . ."

She grabbed the nearest humanitarian award statue from the cardboard box on the nightstand—his less than brilliant method of hiding them out of sight—and held it aloft, squinting at its inscription. Paige had finally spotted the award statues earlier this morning, and he'd briefly explained them, but this time, she appeared to have more than information gathering on her mind.

With a self-important air, Paige drew in a deep breath. She shoved herself a little higher on the pillows, and cleared her throat. She raised the statue still further, then presented it to him with a flourish worthy of a game show hostess.

"For you," she said teasingly. "The world's most thoughtful lover"—a blush highlighted her cheeks—"and most expert teacher."

Brodie accepted the statue, made a pretend bow—at least as much as he could, while straddling a nearly naked, sexy woman—and then set it aside. He frowned. "Teacher? Do you really mean that you've never—"

"Yes!" Paige announced, looking pleased with herself. "Last night was my first time, Brodie. A little unusual these days, I guess, but between studying and working and going on doom dates, I just never found anyone . . . like you. Anyone special enough."

Paige had been a virgin. The real meaning of what they'd shared together struck him then, and Brodie rolled onto his side to pull her close. He held her in his arms, marveling that he'd found a woman as incredible and brilliant and funny as Paige. "I'm honored," he said gruffly. "And I hope it was . . . that you . . . well, that you weren't disappointed."

He felt his face heat. Dammit, had she actually made him blush?

"Disappointed? Heck, no!" Laughing, she stretched languorously at his side, stirring the mussed bed sheets. "I feel terrific. And why shouldn't I? I never dreamed a purely physical experience could be so exciting."

"Oh." Brodie suddenly wished they'd never started talking about this. Half-joking, he said, "Um, you sound like you're only interested in my body."

Paige turned her head to look at him, making her hair swish across the pillows. "Nonsense. Your reputation was an important part of it, too. I just knew you'd be perfect." Sounding giddy, she reached toward the box of award statuettes. "In fact, I think I deserve one of these, too," she said, pulling a gold-plated fellowship award from the pile.

"What for?" Did he really want to know?

Smiling, Paige stroked her hand over the statuette's torso. Then she kissed Brodie. "For excellence in choosing my first real lover, of course."

"Choosing?" He felt an unmistakable chill. "You chose me?"

"Well . . . yes." Confusion wrinkled her brow. "Otherwise, we wouldn't be here. I'm really not the sort of woman who does these things lightly. I had to choose someone, and I—"

Misery turned the rest of her words jumbled and incomprehensible. In shock, he listened to Paige cheerfully explain how she'd selected the famous Brodie Richardson as her introductory lover . . . and knew that he'd been had, all over again.

Despite his hopes, not even steady, dependable Paige Mulvaney had loved him for his mind, his heart, his soul. She'd wanted him for his tabloid reputation and often-photographed body. Nothing more.

The pain of it was too much. He had to get away. With Paige still chattering away, Brodie threw off the sheets and got out of bed, hastily pulling on a pair of black drawstring pants. Their somber color suited his mood perfectly.

She quit talking abruptly. Stared at him. "Where are you going? What's the matter?"

Brodie shrugged. Standing at the foot of the bed, dressed only from the waist down with his hands on his hips, he suddenly seemed much farther away than the few feet that separated them. "Nothing's the matter. I'm just 'choosing' to get out of bed now. Later, I might 'choose' to have breakfast. Maybe even 'choose' to hold a press conference or accept an award."

His dark gaze landed on the statue she clutched lamely in her hand. Feeling foolish, Paige replaced it carefully in the box.

"Life is full of choices," he went on. "Lots of choices."

A prickle of unease made her sit up straighter. Had she said something wrong? She'd been blathering on, Paige knew, too happy and sated and in love to really focus on what she'd been saying. Too giddy, probably, to make much sense at all. So what was Brodie talking about?

"Sure it is," she agreed. In an effort to lighten the suddenly tense mood between them, Paige joked, "Choices like whether to drag you back to bed now, or fortify ourselves with breakfast before attempting to set a new world's record in wonderful lovemaking."

His stoic expression made her wobbly smile vanish as quickly as it appeared. Well, she'd always been about as adept with humor as she'd been with looking sexy—meaning, not adept at all. Last night, though, that hadn't mattered. Brodie had made her feel irresistible and beloved.

"No," he said, his voice husky and filled with some emotion she couldn't name. "You know something? I chose you to be my fiancée for the month."

"You sound like you did that on purpose, or something."

"I did."

Paige froze.

"And why not?" He shrugged, flexing all the muscles in his chest and arms that he'd used to hold her tenderly last night. Pacing, Brodie continued. "You chose me, and I chose you. You were the perfect woman to carry out my plan. You made the phony fiancée scheme twice as believable."

"I-I did?" She didn't like the sound of this at all. Nevertheless, Paige found herself unable to move, unable to stop listening, capable only of shielding herself with the sheet she pulled over her naked, chilly body.

"Sure." Brodie stopped, his back to her. "All my family had to do—all the press had to do—was look at you to know that it had to be true love that brought us together. Because let's face it. It sure wasn't lust at first sight."

Her breath left her. How could he be saying this now? Now, after all they'd shared together? In misery, Paige clutched the sheets against her middle and rocked forward, letting her hair cover her face.

"I needed someone smart," Brodie went on. "Someone smart enough to keep the engagement ruse going. Smart enough not to blab to the press, or get caught by reporters on a date with another man."

Oh, God, Paige realized. *He'd chosen her because of her brains.* He'd chosen her because she'd said she didn't have any other dates to get in the way and bungle up his engagement scheme. He'd chosen her, obviously, because her very plainness made his fake fiancée ruse all that much more believable.

The pain of it rocked her. In that moment, she realized exactly how thoroughly she'd begun to believe that Brodie really wanted her. Really meant the things he'd whispered last night.

I love you, I love you, I love you.

She'd been such a fool. Men said things like that, didn't they, in the midst of lovemaking? They got carried away, told a woman what they thought she wanted to hear. Only the gullible ones believed it. The gullible ones . . . like her.

He hadn't really desired her. Hadn't really been unable to stop, as she'd thought. She'd just been convenient. Another of an undoubtedly long line of women whom he'd flattered and charmed and taken to his bed. He'd probably only made love with her out of pity! Obviously, he didn't think she'd have gotten any other offers.

Near her toes, Brodie's fist tightened on the bed's footboard. Paige glimpsed his white-knuckled grasp in the instant before she turned away, and told herself that at least he'd let her down before she fell any more deeply in love with him.

"That smart woman was you," he finished hoarsely. "Simple as that."

"No. This is what's simple," Paige somehow found the strength to say. "You can take your stupid ring—" She wrenched off the heavy class ring she'd so sentimentally accepted last night and threw it onto the sheets. "And take your ridiculous fiancée scheme, and find somebody else to dodge the reporters with. Because I'm out of the game."

"Fine."

"Fine!"

"I'll leave you alone at the SupraTech employee party on Monday, then," Brodie said, all business.

His face looked haggard, as though he were indescribably sad, or—she had to be reasonable—simply hadn't slept. Well, neither of them had, but she couldn't think about that now.

"If we spend our time talking to other people," he continued, "no one will notice anything is wrong."

"I just told you I'm out of this deal." Bitterness made Paige cross her arms, stubbornly sticking to her guns. "What difference does it make to me if people know our so-called engagement is finished? What makes you think I care what anybody else says?"

He shrugged again. "I can't be the only one with pride."

He was right. Damn him. She had to admit that she'd rather wait until all the SupraTech anniversary celebrations were over with—and she'd quit her temporary assignment as she now planned to do—before publicly splitting with Brodie.

"All right. Then you'll handle the break-up as we agreed." Paige forced herself to concentrate on the business at hand. "A few days after the employee party, with a press release calling it an amicable split?"

"Yes." With a strangely wistful expression, Brodie

picked up the ring she'd yanked off her finger and looked at it. When he finally lifted his gaze to her face, his usually warm hazel eyes were remote. Remote, and almost lonely. "At least we both got what we wanted out of the deal, right?"

"Right." Wrapping the sheets around herself, Paige retrieved her clothes from the floor with as much dignity as possible. "And I even got a bonus."

Brodie's quick glance toward the deserted bed told her he thought she meant their lovemaking had been the 'bonus' she'd spoken of. With an immeasurable sense of loss, Paige decided to set him straight.

"A broken heart," she said. "Shattered and stomped on and then kicked aside. You'd have thought a smart girl like me would have known better."

And then she bundled her clothes in her arms, snatched up her shoes, and disappeared into the bathroom, intent on leaving Brodie's life just as quickly as she'd entered it.

Twelve

Brodie spent most of the SupraTech party wishing he could be anywhere else but there. Frowning, he picked up the latest phone number given to him by a woman in accounting. She'd scrawled it on the back of her business card, adorned it with a flirtatious pink lipstick kiss, and then pushed it into the back pocket of his beachcomber shorts with a come-hither smile.

Brodie wasn't interested. With relish, he fed the card through a paper shredder, watching the strips join those of the first dozen phone numbers he'd received since entering the party. The last thing he wanted was another emotional entanglement.

Another broken heart.

When he looked up again, his mother was approaching. "You might have at least tried to appear vice-presidential, for my sake," Nora Richardson said, surveying his casual shorts, T-shirt, and athletic sandals. "This is a business function, you know."

"I know. But I'm catching a flight to Jamaica right after this. I figured I might as well be ready."

Nora brightened. "Oh! A little romantic getaway

for you and Paige? How nice! Tell me, what does she think of—"

She'd probably think I was running away, Brodie wanted to say, *if she knew I was leaving.* He couldn't stand staying in Saguaro Vista, so near to Paige and still so far away. Going away was for the best. But he was saved by explaining any of that by an announcement from the front of the room.

"Gather round, everyone!" said Pierce, Nora's administrative assistant. "It's time for the special SupraTech awards presentation. First up is Best Use Of Cat Cartoons In Cubicle Decor. And the nominees are . . ."

Groaning, Brodie murmured an excuse to his mother and headed for a quieter corner of the room. He couldn't wait for this damn party and this day to be over with.

From her post beside the ravaged tray of hors d'oeuvres, Paige watched Brodie push his way through the SupraTech partygoers. Sadly, she noticed the stiff set of his shoulders, the grim look on his face, the overall air of sadness that followed him as surely as it did her. For what had to be the millionth time, her heart ached for everything they'd said to each other on that morning a few days—a lifetime—ago.

She'd hurt him. He'd struck back. And now, it was over.

If only Brodie really loved her—loved *all* of her. But he didn't, it seemed. And now, having come so close and having learned so much about herself during the past weeks, Paige couldn't bring herself to settle for less.

But she could, she thought, at least end things on a better note than this. The idea had come to her while watching the endless parade of women approach Brodie at the party, and now was the time to execute it . . . if only she could find the courage.

At the front of the room, Jennifer was walking to the podium, mounting it and accepting her trophy for Employee Most Likely To Inspire A Really Big Hairdo. Laughing, the receptionist raised her award in the air and then made a short speech. When she returned to the crowd again, Paige knew her moment had arrived.

Before her courage could desert her, she wiped her sweaty palms on the skirt of her pale yellow business suit and then rapidly strode to the podium. Once there, Paige looked up.

At the same time, a sea of expectant faces turned toward her. A fresh wave of terror struck, making her knees quake. No wonder, Paige realized in that moment—her first ever in front of a crowd—that public speaking was most people's greatest fear.

"Umm." She cleared her throat and grabbed the microphone, doing her best to force the nervous squeak from her voice. "Well. I have another nomination to make, please."

The crowd quieted. Near the back of the room,

she saw Brodie pause and then turn to face her. *Please understand,* she prayed. *Please listen.*

"It's for someone just about all of you know—but not as well as you think you do." Murmured speculation greeted her announcement, then subsided as she went on speaking. "He's not here very often, and as much as we all wish that weren't true, it's probably for the best. You see, when he's traveling overseas and in the United States, he's not just lolling on a beach or going to parties, as some of us—as I used to—think.

"I recently found out, from a highly reliable source . . ." Paige paused, deciding not to mention Jennifer, who had finally told all. She took a deep breath and went on. "Instead, Brodie volunteered for several charities, around the world and also here at home. He draws on his business experience and unique skills to help causes ranging from wildlife conservation to children's health programs to eco-friendly agriculture. He's using his best assets—a brilliant, innovative mind and a caring heart, to help other people. And for that, no matter how secret he's kept it all this time, I think he should be rewarded."

Paige paused, drawing in a deep breath. She didn't dare look at Brodie. Didn't want to find out how her impromptu announcement had affected him. Instead, she raised one of the SupraTech employee award trophies and finished.

"I propose a new award, and its very first nominee. For Man Of The Year—Brodie Richardson!"

The room burst into applause and cheers. The emcee stepped forward to officially present the unexpected award, and from the corner of her eye, Paige glimpsed Brodie slowly coming forward to accept it. She couldn't face him. Feeling a sudden surge of tears threaten, she pushed her way to the side and made her escape.

"Oh, Paige, don't leave like this!" Jennifer said. She wrung her hands, watching Paige pack her few personal belongings in a box and heft it to the top of her desk. "Don't let Brodie push you out of a job you love, and that you're terrific at."

"He's not pushing me." Resolutely, Paige went on packing. "I'm moving on. It's better this way."

"Oh, hon." In obvious sympathy, Jennifer wrapped her arms around Paige's shoulders and hugged. "Don't you think we all know what you're going through? I've been there."

"Not like this, you haven't."

"But I have. We all have." Leaning conspiratorially forward, Jennifer continued. "I guess I should have warned you beforehand, but I figured you were smarter than the rest of us. Too smart to get yourself hurt by a heartbreaker like him."

"He's not like that," Paige staunchly defended.

"Oh, come on. He's done it to all of us, and I'm sorry he's done it to you now, too." She offered a sympathetic smile. "If it makes you feel any better, you're not alone. It's part of Brodie's mystique. He dates you, makes you feel special and wonderful . . . and then stops just short of the fabulous horizontal mambo you've been hoping for. It's an awful feeling, I know."

Paige stopped, the empty vase she'd used to hold the daily bouquets of flowers that Brodie had sent her clutched in her hand. "Horizontal mambo?"

"You know." Jennifer winked. "Sex. When Brodie refused to sleep with me, I didn't care how easy he let me down. All I wanted was—"

"Refused to sleep with you?"

"Yes. That's what he always does. He must have a policy or something about not getting too cozy with his dates, because—"

"No!" Dropping the vase, Paige stared at Jennifer in amazement. Slowly, what her friend had been trying to tell her sunk in. Brodie *had* desired her. So much so, in fact, that he'd broken his own long-standing rule to be with her. "I've made a terrible mistake."

She turned, determined to find Brodie and set things right before it was too late. She'd only gone a few steps from the cubicle when the sound of his voice stopped her.

"Paige?" he called forlornly. "Paige, are you back here?"

"Brodie?" She caught sight of his head at the far end of the row and started to run to him as he ran to her. At last, they met midway and he handed her a bouquet wrapped in a damask napkin. Some tabletop must be missing its arrange-

MAN OF THE YEAR   169

ment of daisies and carnations and pale pink roses, Paige thought, secretly amused.

"I was such an idiot," Brodie said in a rush. "When I heard you making your speech, I knew I'd jumped to conclusions the other day. When you started talking about my mind, my heart—I knew you saw the real me."

"Oh, Brodie, I was wrong!" Paige cried at the same time. "I didn't know—I didn't realize—oh, I was just afraid to believe that you really wanted me. But now I know"—she darted a glance toward her cubicle, where Jennifer appeared to be *un*packing Paige's box of belongings—"I know that what we had was really special. Is it—is it too late for us?"

"For the Man Of The Year and the woman he loves?" Brodie grinned. "It's never too late. So long as you promise to go wild some of the time—"

"If you promise to continue helping all those wonderful humanitarian projects," Paige interrupted, smiling back as she thought of the secret foundation he'd established for his charity work.

"Okay. If you promise to consider this"—Brodie dropped to one knee, pulling something small and square from his surfer-style baggy shorts—"then it will never, never, be too late. I'm sorry for all the misunderstandings, Paige. Please say you'll be mine."

He whipped a brown paper sack from behind his back and offered it to her. "And please say you'll take these, too," he added. "I know how much you love the little courtesies of dating, but

I couldn't find the traditional box of chocolates on such short notice. So I hope these will do."

Paige opened the sack and peered down at the assortment of party hors d'oeuvres contained inside. She laughed, feeling giddy enough to turn cartwheels at the look of passionate love on Brodie's face, and at his endearing insistence on giving her all the things he thought she wanted . . . when all she really needed was him. "We'll want something to keep our strength up on the honeymoon, after all."

He studied her for a long moment, then gave her another smile. "Did you just wink at me?"

"Actually, I think I just proposed to you." Bravely, Paige wrapped her arms around his neck, waist-high because of his on-bended-knee position. "Yes, I'm certain I did."

"Then why am I the one holding this?"

Brodie raised his hand, revealing the box he'd retrieved from his pocket . . . now opened to display the diamond and sapphire engagement ring tucked inside. Paige gasped.

"I love you with all my heart," he told her quietly. "Please, Paige . . . say you'll marry me."

"I will!" she cried, blinking back the tears—tears of happiness, now—that threatened to fall. "I love you, too, Brodie. More than I can say."

And then Paige got on her knees before the man of her dreams, hugged him tight, and proceeded to show him, with actions *and* words, exactly how much. Together, they held each other close, and knew that finally, everything would be all right.

After all, things definitely had a way of working out for Paige Mulvaney—and for Brodie Richardson, too. There was no doubt about it.

ABOUT THE AUTHOR

"I feel lucky to have the greatest job on earth," Lisa Plumley says, "creating stories I hope will touch readers' hearts, spark their imaginations . . . and tickle their funny bones, too." Her work includes short contemporary romances, western historical romances, and time-travel romances, all written from her home in sunny Arizona, where she lives with her husband and two children.

Lisa loves to hear from readers! You can write to her c/o P.O. Box 7105, Chandler, AZ 85246-7105, send e-mail to *lisa@lisaplumley.com,* or visit Lisa on the internet at *http:www.lisaplumley.com.* Happy reading!